"I'm not asking you to marry me...."

"And I don't even think we should live together," Leon continued. "I'm just saying you should move back to Alaska because it's better for you. I want you to be happy, and I think we can, well, see each other."

"See each other?" Casey repeated.

"You know I've always told you that I'm not a marrying kind of guy," he told her.

"So let me get this straight," she said. "I'm supposed to give up my chance to work for one of the finest universities in the country and move back to Alaska, all so that I can 'see' you at your convenience?"

"I'm telling you I think there's something between us," he said quietly. "Something that makes me want you even when I think you're the most irritating woman ever placed on the face of the earth."

"And I think," she said, her voice cold and prim, "that you have all the qualities I have *never* wanted in a man!"

Dear Reader,

October is a very special month at Silhouette Romance. We're celebrating the most precious love of all...a child's love. Our editors have selected five heartwarming stories that feature happy-ever-afters with a family touch—*Home for Thanksgiving* by Suzanne Carey, *And Daddy Makes Three* by Anne Peters, *Casey's Flyboy* by Vivian Leiber, *Paper Marriage* by Judith Bowen and *Beloved Stranger* by Peggy Webb.

But that's not all! We're also continuing our WRITTEN IN THE STARS series. This month we're proud to present one of the most romantic heroes in the zodiac—the Libra man—in Patricia Ellis's *Pillow Talk*.

I hope you enjoy this month's stories, and in the months to come, watch for Silhouette Romance novels by your all-time favorites, including Diana Palmer, Brittany Young, Annette Broadrick and many others.

The authors and editors of Silhouette Romance books strive to bring you the best of romance fiction, stories that capture the laughter, the tears—the sheer joy—of falling in love. Let us know if we've succeeded. We'd love to hear from you!

Happy Reading,

Valerie Susan Hayward
Senior Editor

VIVIAN LEIBER

Casey's Flyboy

Silhouette Romance

Published by Silhouette Books New York

America's Publisher of Contemporary Romance

To Stephen

SILHOUETTE BOOKS
300 E. 42nd St., New York, N.Y. 10017

CASEY'S FLYBOY

ISBN: 0-373-08822-1

First Silhouette Books printing October 1991

Printed in the U.S.A.

VIVIAN LEIBER

began writing stories when she was ten years old. Girlfriends passed around notebooks filled with her handwritten romantic adventures in which such teen idols as Bobby Sherman, David Cassidy and the safety-patrol boy in the eighth grade figured prominently. Grown up now, and living with a husband, two stepchildren and her own two-year-old son, Vivian finds romance ficiton to be the best antidote to the type of frazzled day that every working mother has.

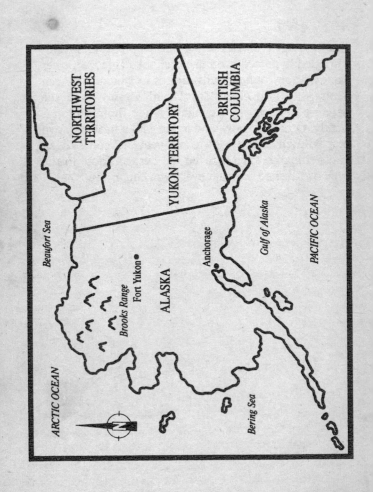

Chapter One

The first pain came at eleven, startling Casey awake. With clenched teeth and progressively deeper fingernail digs into her palms, she waited out that first and then a second seemingly endless grip of pain. She slept in between the contractions, unwilling to give in to panic because the day, spent cleaning baby clothes and tidying the nursery, had been exhausting. She wanted to sleep, not to be thrust into the primal battle that baby and mother face at the dawn of new life.

At each contraction, third, fourth and more—until she lost track—she stared at the nightstand clock, watching the second hand sweep in a circle. She breathed deeply, letting her mind remain unfocused, waiting for the pain to subside. Each contraction lasted precisely one minute, just as Dr. Holt had said it would. The cramping—didn't it feel better to think of them as cramps instead of as contractions?—was spaced twenty, then fifteen, then ten minutes apart and it became more difficult to fool herself, to persuade herself that it wasn't time.

She didn't want to face the prospect of real labor and she didn't want to face the embarrassment of another false alarm, another embarrassing rush to a hospital fifty miles away, across the frigid snows. A trip that would end with a nurse patting her on the wrist and telling her to go home and relax.

So she waited, letting eleven become midnight, midnight become one, and one slip away to two. Waited and listened drowsily to the men at the bar below—bragging and boasting and topping each other's stories and slipping into comradely songs.

Just before four, her water broke—a sudden, involuntary rush of liquid down her legs. Casey had to face the truth. She pulled herself out of bed, struggling with the heavy, swollen hardness that was her own belly. She smiled ruefully as she launched herself into an upright position. Having gained twenty pounds during the pregnancy, most of it in the final two months, she still found it hard to believe this was her body, and not some extraordinary practical joke.

When she switched on the nightstand lamp, a soft, pink, warm glow enveloped the room. She picked up the small framed photograph resting on the table and smiled at the image of the serious-looking man who stood next to a blackboard in front of a classroom of students. Another contraction squeezed her stomach, spreading a belt of pain all around her back. The last one was only five minutes before, she thought, her hands shakily returning the photograph to its position on the table.

She shoved herself off the bed, yanking the peach flannel nightgown over her stomach. Her feet searched the floor for her slippers—there was no use in trying to bend over, she hadn't been able to actually see or touch her feet for a month. Casey pulled on a terry robe and looped its belt beneath her enormous belly.

Nothing had prepared her for the birth of her baby. With no husband to lean on for support, she had denied the very fact of her pregnancy until the last trimester, and even then she had ignored her doctor's advice to learn Lamaze and to take in extra calories, refusing to slack off in the work around the cabin and on the field expeditions to Athabascan Indian villages. She determinedly squeezed her ever-larger body into oversize sweaters and stretch pants until, at last, in her eighth month, she had broken down and taken to wearing her dead husband's sweaters. She had started to eat in those last eight weeks, overcoming the grief that had made every bite taste like cardboard.

Eat for your baby, she had told herself—eat for his baby.

Another contraction was coming, she knew, gripping the brass footboard of her bed. Her desire to run away, to hide, to escape into the bristling cold Alaskan night was checked by the knowledge that it was her body that was holding her hostage.

"Skip!" She cried out, hoping her voice would carry over the strains of a half-dozen drunken fur trappers and bush pilots downstairs singing a sixteenth chorus of "Louie Louie." "Skip! Hurry!"

She propelled herself to the small wing chair next to the door of her room, throwing aside the half-finished text of anthropology abstracts that she had studied only that evening. An abrupt, eerie end to the singing and a heavy pounding of boots on the stairs told her that help was on its way.

Through the open door, a grizzled elf of a man appeared. He was nearly as small as Casey, with round wire-rimmed glasses, pixielike ears and a shiny bald head sprinkled with tiny tufts of white hair. He was dressed in a blue plaid flannel shirt, and a hint of his long underwear showed at his collar and at the worn patches on his elbows.

"Skip, the contractions—they're coming too close," Casey exclaimed breathlessly. She raised her sapphire-blue eyes to meet his concerned gaze. "I don't think we're going to make it to the hospital. I waited so long, thinking it might be another false alarm...."

"But it's early," Skip said, helping her into a comfortable sitting position. "Doctor said you weren't due for two weeks, and even then, first-time moms go a couple of weeks past their due date. This isn't another false alarm, is it?"

She shook her head, fighting the pincer-grip of pain. Out of the corner of her eye, she could see four or five men somberly staring through the bedroom door. The mood of celebration had evaporated; Alaskans bred on independence and an unfriendly climate learn to treat each emergency as their own.

"Skip, you want to explain to the baby that he's early?" she gasped through clenched teeth.

Not needing to be told twice, and startled by the uncharacteristically irritable tone of her voice, he turned to the men at the door.

"I know none of you guys are M.D.s, but do any of you know how to help out a birth?"

A few of the men shook their heads and stared at the ground. If anyone had said yesterday that she'd let Skip's customers help with her baby, Casey would have told them no thanks. Funny what pain can do to a woman, she thought grimly. Dr. Holt had told her that women in labor lost all sense of modesty—the desperate struggle to give birth outweighing all other concerns. The stories of women having babies in taxis, on airplanes and in elevators, with the help of total strangers, had meant nothing to Casey.

Until now.

"I once helped a woman at Kodiak," an unfamiliar male voice said, as the men at the door made way for a short, bespectacled man. Casey remembered him as being a flyboy—one of the many pilots in Alaska, so necessary to everyday life—willing to fly anyone anywhere for a price. He must have seen the look of skepticism that crossed her face, because he added, "Twins. Woman named them after me. My name's Calvin Dodge, so she named one twin Calvin and the other—"

"Fine, you're hired." Skip impatiently cut him off.

The men at the door began to drift quietly down the stairs, back to the bar.

"Wait," Calvin demanded, efficiency and command coming to him. "I'll need some help. Skip, I want you to boil me some water and find me some clean, washed cloth. And Leon, I want you to help me with the lady."

Slouched casually against the doorjamb, a tall, black-haired pilot, a man who, in Casey's befogged state, looked like nothing more than an inverted pyramid of muscle, shook his head. Casey had only seen him briefly before, as he and Calvin had tossed back a few beers. She remembered him as the one the other men had toasted early in the evening for his role in flying in to save a blizzard-bound group of pipeline workers just the week before. Sitting in the bar by the fireplace, reading through anthropological texts, she had been startled to find herself studying him, even as her baby seemed to do somersaults in her abdomen.

"Calvin, I can't help with a—" Leon started to protest, with just a hint of a slow, southern drawl.

"You have to walk her around," Calvin ordered, as both Leon and Casey stared at him in disbelief.

"I'm going to have a baby and I'm in pain," Casey cried out, hating the whining tone of her voice, but utterly unable to stop it. When Dr. Holt said that labor was the most painful experience a human could endure, she knew what she was talking about. "I want something for the pain—not an exercise class."

"Walking will make the baby move faster," Calvin explained. "That's what you want—a faster delivery. Having a baby isn't like in the movies, where you lay in bed in a silk jacket. It's hard work and you need to use every advantage you can get."

The three—Calvin, Leon, and Casey—were stalemated for a moment, each unwilling or unable to budge. Skip broke the silence by announcing he was going downstairs to boil water, and the remaining hangers-on at the door followed him.

"I'm going to get things ready for the baby," Calvin said quietly. "Just make sure that you walk up and down the hallway, stopping only when the pain is too much. Leon, keep track of the time in between contractions. When it's down to a minute or so, make sure Skip and I are up here." He headed for the door but glanced back once at Casey. "One other thing—if you get the urge to push, call me."

Leon and Casey stared at each other silently after Calvin disappeared. She wasn't quite sure why, but she didn't like him, something about his cool maleness—maybe it was simply the fact that he wasn't in pain and she was. The nurse at Dr. Holt's office told Casey that when she had been in labor, she had taken off her wedding and engagement rings and thrown them at her husband—all because she was in so much pain and her husband wasn't.

Casey blinked harshly—another contraction.

"It'll be better if you don't hold your breath," Leon advised, his voice irritating even as it soothed.

Casey was about to protest that she wasn't holding her breath, but then realized he was right. She gulped at the air, tightening her fingers around the cotton chintz of the chair's upholstery. He sat down at her feet, gently pulling her hand into his own.

"Hey, it's going to be all right," he said.

She jerked her hand away, and just as the pain subsided, struggled to her feet. She didn't want his hand in hers, she didn't want his emerald-green eyes meeting her own, she didn't want his tenderness that threatened the wall of independence that had been forged by tragedy eight months before.

"He said to walk, so let's just do it."

Leon bit his lip, nearly ready to snap back at her. Then he remembered helping his father to birth calves and colts in the small, Alabama barn out back of his home. Some of the animals had gotten mighty irrational and testy, Leon reminded himself as he followed her out into the hallway. As a flyboy who flew to whatever Alaskan emergency beckoned, Leon had often held a life in his hands, a life that depended on his quick thinking, resourcefulness and a steady, calm strength. Having long ago learned to rein in his emotions during a crisis, Leon was surprised now at the feelings that swelled within him. He had been aware of the mysterious woman since he first strolled into Skip's Place. He had been embarrassed by the cheers of the men over his rescue of the pipeline workers and had covertly looked over at this woman as she studied by the fireplace, trying to measure her reactions, trying to understand her.

For a moment, he had thought it was simple attraction, although clearly more powerful than anything he had felt before. *Get a grip on yourself,* Leon had thought when she had stood up and he realized that she was pregnant. Though he had told himself that there was a husband somewhere, he now wondered where the father-to-be was.

But he knew enough not to ask.

They paced the pinewood floor for forty-five minutes, Casey stopping when a contraction began. At first, she bristled at the stranger's efforts to hold her arm or brush a comforting hand across her sweat-soaked hair as she closed her eyes in a vain effort to alleviate the pain. She slapped him away when he tried to put his arm around her shoulder to hold her up as she doubled over. The contractions were coming every two minutes, with Casey barely able to compose herself, take a few steps, catch her breath—and be shoved into another tormenting minute of unbelievable agony.

And, suddenly, the contractions stopped. Nothing. No pain. As if her body had capitulated.

She looked up at Leon, for the first time taking in the calm green of his eyes. She didn't know whether to be worried or relieved and looked to him for some clue.

"It's over," she said, tentatively smiling. "It's over."

He didn't have the heart to tell her that the real work was only just beginning, that everything up to that point was nothing compared to what would follow. He put his arms around her, surprised to feel the frailness of her shoulders and arms, wondering briefly at the circumstances of this birth and at the grief that was so evident on her face, noticeable even when he had first entered the firelit bar that afternoon and had seen her seated at a corner table, herbal tea in hand, studying and writing with seemingly unshakable concentration.

She did not resist, but entered gratefully into his embrace, happy to believe that she had been given a reprieve. Her mind was clearing—she could forget that only moments before, she had been convinced she was on the brink of death, that she would never see her baby, that her body was exploding from the pressures within.

"Oh, God," she said suddenly, with a despondency that immediately alerted Leon.

"What is it?" he asked, already knowing as she sagged ever so slightly in his arms.

She lifted her flushed, damp face.

How could she describe it to him? How could she tell him that it felt as if the baby had positioned himself, ready to alight, ready to stretch out his arms and reach for the world? And that same inner mechanism, utterly at her baby's control, was ready now—to split her body in two, if necessary, to rocket into the world?

"I'm ready," she said simply.

With a strength she couldn't have believed was possible, Leon picked her up and carried her into the bedroom, laying her gently on the soft mattress. When he called for Skip and Calvin, she took one last look at the picture by the bed, the picture of the man who should have been here, the man whose hand she should have held.

Two grueling hours later, a baby's scream joined her own. She felt her hand slip from Leon's, and she watched as he and Skip proudly, reverently, helped Calvin to cut the cord.

"It's a boy!" Skip shouted excitedly. "Drinks all around! On the house. Bar's open." He ran to the door of the bedroom and repeated his news. A spontaneous cheer erupted from the men. Calvin, exhausted, announced he needed a drink and disappeared after a moment's disappointment when Casey whispered that her son's name was to be Joseph, his dead father's middle name.

Leon held the baby out to her, staring at him with a look of awe, as if it were his own. She looked down at her son, surprised at his alert and somewhat suspicious stare.

"I wasn't very brave, was I?" she asked, remembering Leon had held her hand and encouraged her for the hours of pushing and recovering, pushing and recovering.

"No, I have to admit, you're a whiner and a complainer," he said. "I've never seen someone so irritable."

She smiled. Dr. Holt had said that no matter how bad the pain was, she had yet to meet a woman who didn't forget all the pain as soon as the baby was born. Casey was no exception. Suddenly it seemed to have been an easy labor. Especially now that she saw her baby boy.

"He's beautiful, isn't he?" Casey asked.

"They always are, love," Skip answered, coming round to sit on the other side of the bed.

Skip took him from her and wrapped a dish towel tightly around the boy, encasing the flailing arms and legs like a sausage.

"They like to be bundled up tight," Skip explained. "They get out of the womb and suddenly there's all this room to fling their arms around. Makes them think their legs and arms are going to fly away."

She wondered where he had acquired his knowledge of babies. He had never struck her as a baby person. Until now—when he held the dark-haired baby to his chest.

Don't get too attached to this baby, Skip, she thought, wistfully smiling at his attentions to her son. *We have to leave soon,* Casey silently reminded him. *We have to go home.*

She took her baby from Skip's arms and let him snuggle into the safety of her arms.

"Would it be all right if I went downstairs?" Skip asked. "I mean, I'll leave the door open and everything. It's just the boys . . . they're kind of anxious to celebrate."

"Me, too," Leon announced, returning to the stance of relaxed masculinity that he found natural. "I'm getting a little stir-crazy in here."

She looked up at Leon and, for a brief instance, thought she felt regret at his leaving. Something had been forged between them, something that seemed too strong to simply walk away from. When her eyes met his for a brief instant, she thought that he felt that bond, that strength, that regret as well. Perhaps he did, because seeing his eyes, she sensed that he had opened up to her in the past hours in a way that he found difficult to let go of, difficult to surrender.

With an embarrassed and flustered half smile, he gently touched the baby's head and, without another word, left the room.

Skip followed him, and she was left alone with her son.

"I love you," she whispered to the sleeping baby, glancing briefly at the photograph on the nightstand. "You're all I have left of him. Of your daddy."

She closed her eyes, and giving one last, tender squeeze to her baby, gave herself up to a deep, long-awaited sleep. She dreamed of a beautiful home, far away, with cascading chandeliers and cozy armchairs, a brilliant green lawn and gardens of pastel flowers, happy children and an adoring husband. It was a home she dreamed of often. It was a home that had never existed.

Downstairs, the celebratory mood of the men at Skip's bar had suddenly, without warning, collapsed into dark, grim contemplation. The hurrahs said, the toasts made and drunk, the one chorus of "For He's a Jolly Good Fellow" over, the men, even Skip, were quiet and inexplicably sober. All the men—except Calvin.

"What's wrong with you guys?" he chirped as he wiped his glasses with Skip's dish towel. "There's new life upstairs. It should be making us think of optimism and hope and new beginnings."

There was a long pause as the men stared at Calvin. Leon could have kicked his friend, thinking that someone might start an argument. Instead, one man shook his head and stared back into his drink.

"I played around on my old lady for a few years, always telling her I needed my freedom," he explained to no one and yet, to everyone. "Then, one day, she said she wasn't going to take it anymore, told me to pack my bags. At first I thought it was great, running around, not tied down by the wife and baby—then I realized I was lonely for her. Hah! Freedom."

"And then what happened?" Calvin asked as he put on his glasses, making his face look like that of an owl.

"I went back to her, begging her forgiveness—even brought her flowers—and she told me she had found someone new. There's another man out there that my kid calls Dad and my wife calls husband."

"Oh," Calvin said, at last aware that he had steered the conversation in the wrong direction.

The gloomy silence fell back over the room.

"Dammit, I propose a toast," Leon commanded, raising his beer with a bravado he wasn't sure he felt. But he knew he had to do something to take the sullen crowd's attention away from his bumbling friend. "To women!"

The toast wasn't one of his better ideas—he realized there were seven sets of eyes trained on him, seven men who, for whatever reason, didn't agree with him in the slightest.

"We love them," he continued, feeling the need to put into words his feelings about the evening. "We love them, we want them, we need them."

The men looked at each other—and the bitter truth of their lonely condition didn't amuse them. Skip broke the mood.

"To women," he announced, raising his own coffee cup with a gesture that broached no disagreement. "We love them because we are incomplete without them."

The men hurrahed and downed their drinks, and in an unspoken agreement to banish their bleak thoughts, turned the conversation to the recent prices on deer and fox skins.

Leon watched the men, unshaven and as uncivilized as any he met in the course of his flights through the Alaskan countryside. Smiling occasionally to give the appearance of keeping up with the conversation, he thought of his comrades. Was it really the life he wanted twenty years from now, when he was in his fifties, to be alone in a bar, to sit always in the company of new faces, in a life as solitary as theirs?

And then, without even knowing the answer to that question, he asked himself another. Was he ready to trade on that freedom, to give it up? He thought of the woman upstairs, and the few hours when he had felt part of a drama much larger than his own life. Others had depended on him. In fact, his whole life, he had been a man with the strength that made others place their lives in his hands. But when this woman depended on him, he felt that he was getting something back, some extraordinary gift of love and trust. The notion frightened him, threatening as it was to his independence, an independence that had grown in Alaska's harsh climate until it had the strength of the muskegon—the state's hardy, pervasive moss.

"This is just one more exciting paragraph in the great Leon Brodie legend," Calvin said, sliding onto the bar stool next to Leon. "Every time I turn around, you're doing something heroic."

"Yeah, but you're the one who knew what he was doing," Leon chided, and poured Calvin another beer from the pitcher that Skip had left on the bar.

"Nobody will remember I was even here," Calvin said, shrugging off Leon's comment. "But what do I care? I'm already married, so I don't need women falling all over themselves like you have 'em."

Leon unconsciously looked over at the fireplace, its flames banked down to a red glow, the fireplace where she had sat. Her books and notepad, teacup and pens were still stacked on the table nearest to the embers.

"Let's get some sleep and hurry on out of here," he commanded gruffly.

Chapter Two

Forcefully thrown by a ferocious, whistling wind, afternoon snowflakes blanketed the ground. Clouds that had formed over the Brooks mountain range only hours before had brought a harsh, unexpected September storm. The solitary Land Rover's wheels spun uselessly, incapable of passing through the foothills that surrounded northeastern Alaskan mountains.

Casey shifted into second gear and shoved her boot down on the accelerator. The wheels of the Land Rover dug farther into the bank of snow. *It's just an early fall storm*, she reassured herself. *Surely nothing to worry about.* In this portion of Alaska, serious snows didn't start until early October; spring didn't melt the ice until nearly June.

Above the Arctic Circle, there were winter days when the sun didn't pierce the horizon and the temperature hovered near fifty degrees—*below zero.* But even in this innermost part of Alaska, there were summer days when the mercury nearly hit seventy.

Those days, those few summer days, were long gone, taking aqua-blue skies and brilliant sunshine with them. And, thankfully, the mosquitoes, Casey thought wryly, echoing the sentiments of many Alaskans.

This afternoon storm, sudden and without warning, was an ominous reminder of the supremacy of nature and of her tyranny in the coming months.

Casey reminded herself that she was leaving—and wouldn't be battling another Alaskan winter. She had other plans—plans that had been set in stone even before Joseph had been born, before Robert had died. Setting up a museum exhibit of Athabascan Indian artifacts at the University of Chicago was the culmination of her and her husband's work and represented her ticket to the Outside—what a native smugly referred to as anything that wasn't Alaska.

Casey couldn't wait to get to Chicago. To plant her feet on a real sidewalk—most Alaskan roads and sidewalks were gravel because the extreme temperatures destroyed concrete. To go to a real play, not one of the amateur performances put on in school gymnasiums at Fort Yukon. To eat in a restaurant, instead of relying on Skip's "experiments."

Mostly, though, she wanted to prove herself in her work, to put together the pieces of her anthropological research and see if it added anything to the complex and diverse field.

Besides, somehow she thought the exhibit would release Robert's hold on her, an embrace she wasn't entirely sure she wanted to let go of, yet a grip that made her uneasy.

During the exhibit's month-long run at the university's museum, she would be treated as a professional, and during the interview and lectures she would be giving to promote the exhibit, she would be looked upon to explain all facets of Athabascan life. The whole idea made her queasy, as if she couldn't quite believe that she had a degree in anthropology or had spent nearly two years studying the tribe.

And after the exhibit was over, and the artifacts consigned to the Native American section of the museum?

She wasn't sure of the details, but she wanted to remain Outside, in Chicago, working for the university. Chicago had been the first place she had settled down, after a tumultuous childhood spent in what seemed like a whirlwind routine of moving from house to house. For Casey, the university, with its emphasis on the mind, on thoughtful inquiry, on studied and reasoned research, was forever linked with a sense of safety and security—a safety and security that a wild and untamed Alaska could never offer.

Yes, Chicago would be a nice place to call home, she thought, savoring the image of energy and vitality, the cultural advantages and the warmth of the city, and not even considering that her memory may be faulty, that she may have felt as uncomfortable and lonely when she had lived as a college student in Chicago as she did now in Alaska as a widow.

Snow and ice slammed against the windshield, the force of the wind enough to shake the hearty four-wheel-drive vehicle. Casey's stomach churned with fear. This must have been what it was like for Robert during those last hours, she thought. The panic, the darkness, the disbelief at nature's supremacy.

The snows wouldn't claim another life...or would they? She set her jaw determinedly and nudged the accelerator again.

"Come on, baby," she whispered, thinking of her six-month-old son. "Joseph will wonder what's happened to me."

The Land Rover protested, groaning as she rocked it gently with a persistent *tap-tap-tap* on the pedals. At last, its wheels slid over the slippery road. Casey was grateful, as were so many before her, for the added traction that gravel road provided. She relaxed her shoulders and let out a barely audible "thanks."

Guiding the Land Rover through the unbroken fields and craggy hills of white, she paused when she arrived at a wide-open valley nestled between a ridge of foothills. Bathed with light by late-afternoon sun, a cabin stood near a fold of blue spruce trees, shining like a Christmas ornament. A single-engine, two-seater plane was parked only a hundred feet from the wood structure. The pilot she had hired from Calvin Dodge's transport service must have arrived!

The Land Rover, seemingly as excited about getting home as she, roared over the snow. In no time, Casey parked a few feet from the cabin and jumped from her vehicle. Playfully licking the first clean-tasting snowflakes that dropped onto her lips, she smiled. Then, responding to her need to see her baby son, she pulled a wood crate from the trunk and hoisted it onto her shoulders.

Over the front door of the cabin was the small, wood-carved sign that proclaimed Skip's Place—hotel at the top of the world. Struggling under the heavy box, she kicked at the door and it was quickly opened.

"Hi, Skip, I've got some beaded hides in here. I'll show you." She struggled past him into the wood-paneled room that served as lobby, tavern, restaurant and living room. It boasted all the amenities: a fireplace, a few tables, an upright piano and a bar that stretched the full length of the room.

And there was something extra most bars don't have—a playpen filled with toys. Most of the toys had been made by hand. Skip had carved wooden blocks and many of the regulars who passed through had, at one time or another, brought a little present for Joseph.

A blast of hot, smoky air from the brilliant fire scorched Casey's frozen rose-colored cheeks.

"Any more out there?" Skip asked, quickly slamming the door behind her.

Casey let the crate slide to the floor and pulled the hood of her parka, causing a bob of gently curled chestnut hair to fall onto her face. The fireplace sputtered and crackled, and it sent a rush of needed warmth through her body.

"No, nothing else," she replied, shaking her head. "That's all I could get today. How's my favorite little boy?"

"Joseph's right there," Skip said, pointing across the room to the round, rag-weave rug in front of the glowing fireplace. On the rug, covered by a light blue blanket, lay a sleeping baby. "He's been wonderful today—just went down, as a matter of fact. I was playing him ragtime on the piano. Those new music sheets you mailed away for are just great."

Casey pulled off her parka and dropped it to the floor, uncovering gray jeans snugly covering boyishly slim hips. She stared at her baby for a minute, struck as she was each time she saw him how beautiful he was, how perfectly plump his cheeks, how unblemished his tenderly pink skin, how soft his gingerbread-colored hair.

He's mine, she thought with fierce pride. *He is everything to me.* She brushed her hair away from her face, and passing the long bar, sank into one of the cushioned chairs by the fireplace. As the muscles in her shoulders relaxed, she realized what a long day it had been, rushing from tribal settlement to settlement, gathering the woven baskets and moose hides that the Athabascan Indians were willing to let a far-off museum keep. How good it was to be back home, with her child—she could stare at Joseph forever, and she watched every breath, every twitch of his fingers with adoration. In a silence broken only by the occasional crackle and hiss of the fire, she listened attentively to her baby's soft snores.

Get a grip on yourself, she thought. *You're proud of a baby simply because he snores?*

Knowing the answer, she reluctantly turned her attention to Skip, who had brushed the snow from her parka and was now standing behind the empty bar.

"You're wonderful to Joseph," she said, not for the first time grateful to this man who acted as grandfather, babysitter, confidant and cook. Some people found Skip a little rough: many only saw the blustery man with a penchant for liquor and swearing a blue streak. It seemed that Casey was the only one who knew he was a gentle, softspoken man who would spend hours playing peekaboo or patty cake with her son. Luckily there were seldom any guests at the six-room hotel during the fall and winter months. Casey and Joseph had Skip all to themselves and could depend on his rough-hewn tenderness. "I don't know what we'd do without you."

"Stop the sweet talk," Skip barked, reluctant to acknowledge his own need to be with the young woman and her baby. "You want a cup of coffee or what?"

He pulled off the dish towel that lay across his shoulder and slapped it down on the bar. Coffee and beer, whiskey and scotch—those were the only drinks Skip dispensed.

Casey had found that, with her small frame, she was lucky if she could drink a whole bottle of beer without passing out or acting silly. She still cringed whenever Skip teased her about the time she sang the score from Puccini's *La Bohème* for a group of trappers passing through, and after only two beers!

A cup of coffee sounded good—and harmless.

"I need a hot bath, too," she said, nodding as he poured a cup of his fragrant coffee. "It's already so cold out there. Only a few days before I have to be in Chicago."

Skip held the cup of coffee out to her.

"Speaking of Chicago, your pilot is here," he said, sitting on the couch across from her and propping his spindly legs on the coffee table.

Casey sat straight in her chair. For the first time since she came into the cabin, her blue eyes sparkled with excitement. She held her fist up to her chest, alarmed by the acceleration of her heartbeat.

Was it the stranger? she wondered, remembering the dark-haired man who had helped her when Joseph had been born. When she had called the transport company owned by Calvin Dodge—dear Calvin, who had left forty or fifty business cards at the bar and didn't seem to understand that most of the people who came to Skip's didn't know what to make of them—she had wondered if the flyboy he would send would be the same.

She had been surprised and curiously disappointed, when she had discovered that he had left with Calvin the very day Joseph had been born, without even a goodbye. And she thought of him often, surprisingly attracted to the memory of his comforting arms when she had been in pain, and the special bond they had shared at the moment of Joseph's birth. Each time her thoughts had been drawn to him, she had remembered—guiltily, shamefully—that she had been Robert's bride, that she had shared his bed and borne his child.

She closed her eyes and brought to mind the image of her dead husband, Robert, who had brought her here, who had offered protection and comfort, who had tried . . .

But the image of that older man, a man with a patient and intelligent face, had grown dimmer in her mind, and it took more and more concentration to bring his features into focus.

She opened her eyes, startled to see Skip staring at her intently.

"That's wonderful news," she exclaimed. "But maybe I don't know enough about planes. Wasn't that a two-seater out there?"

"Yup."

"But isn't that a little small? It would have room for him and me and nothing else. I told Calvin that I needed it to transport me and about four hundred pounds of artifacts. And Joseph."

"Yup," Skip replied, shrugging as he looked into the fire.

"Calvin told me he'd send someone who could take everything," Casey continued, her voice rising. *Don't panic,* she told herself. "How could he think a two-seater would do it? He didn't tell me what kind of plane he had, but—"

"Your pilot is out there now if you want to talk to him," Skip said quietly. "He's working on the plane. You've got to be at the university with that exhibit in a week. At this point, Calvin's got you in a tight squeeze—not that he meant to. After all, you need to leave by day after tomorrow if you're going to get there in time for the opening."

She turned away from him and stared into the fireplace, now uncertain whether she was disappointed or angry at Calvin.

Or whether she was angry at the stranger—she knew only his first name, Leon—the man who seemed to threaten her stable life.

Don't think about feelings now, she commanded herself. Instead she tried to focus on the problems posed by the exhibit.

The only money she had coming in was the honorarium the school was giving her for the lecture she would give on the opening day of the exhibit. She was willing to use the honorarium for transporting the artifacts, and she was grateful to Calvin that he was willing to send a plane up for her at such a reduced rate—especially after she told him that she had put Joseph's middle name as "Calvin" on his birth certificate. But a two-seater plane wasn't big enough, and she wasn't sure she could call Calvin and tell him that because she didn't want to appear ungrateful.

Damn you, Robert, why did you leave me? she thought, frightened by the anger she sometimes felt toward her husband. For dying—as if he'd wanted it.

She sipped the hot, rich coffee as her thoughts returned to the past.

Robert Stevens had been her first-year anthropology professor, teaching a course in North American Indian culture. She had been attracted to anthropology because it seemed to be a discipline that could explain human behavior—and to an orphan who had been buffeted from one reluctant relative to another for most of her life, human behavior was an utter mystery.

Bowled over by Robert's encyclopedic mind and the passion he brought to his subject, she quickly selected anthropology as her major. She worked closely with him, taking all his classes, spending weekends in Regenstein library doing research and signing up for all his classes.

Vacations she spent with the perennial group of students who followed him to the Northwest for fieldwork. For four years she spent Thanksgiving and Christmas with that group. But then, Casey knew, there hadn't been any other place to go. The bitterness of the memories of Christmases and Thanksgivings spent with unwilling relatives had long since disappeared. Robert's crowd had been almost like having a family—a loving family. It had been enough for her.

She had shared nothing more personal with Robert than a late-night cup of coffee at a camp fire when other research assistants dropped off to sleep. While other single professors were frequently dogged by rumors of romances with students, Robert was somehow immune. Maybe it was his manner, somewhat aloof and cold. Maybe it was because he never joked, maintaining a rigid exterior that seemed to broach no intimate approach. Nothing tampered with his reputation as an utterly professional teacher.

Then there was the spring afternoon in her senior year. They were at his office, reviewing some tapes of Athabascan Indian storytellers; it was the first time she had been asked to work with him alone. He told her of his dream to master and record their culture before it was destroyed by continued contact with civilization. He mentioned he was one-eighth Athabascan, though he had never lived in Alaska.

"I'd like to begin work this summer," he said as they sat at his desk reviewing the transcripts. "I have a year's research leave coming up and I have a grant from the federal government. I even have a friend, his name's Skip—he owns a hotel he's willing to let me use as a base camp."

"It sounds wonderful," she replied, preoccupied with concern about her own summer, after graduation, after her scholarship money ran out. She would be twenty-two, with a degree from one of the best universities in the country. She had spent four years working so hard to insure her graduation that she hadn't had time to come up for air, to consider the rest of her life. The school had become a safe haven, a home to a girl who didn't have one. What would she do next? Even though she would be graduating at the top of her class, she didn't know.

"It would be a long, tough project," Robert continued, his eyes narrowing as they focused on her. "Some of their lands are inaccessible except by air. I'd need a good research assistant, someone unafraid of some hardship."

"Just one?" Casey asked, puzzled. Ordinarily Robert took five or six assistants on field expeditions.

"Yes," he replied, and held out his hand across the desk to her. "I'm sorry, Casey. I feel like a schoolboy using any ploy he can to get the girl—I'm not very good with women."

"You want to go out with me?" Casey asked. If he wanted an affair with her, she wasn't sure what to say. Though she had spent much of the past four years with him, she hadn't noticed before that he was attractive, with a touch of gray at his temples and a pleasant crinkle at his eyes.

But what did a date have to do with Alaska?

"I'd like you to come with me, as my wife," he said, interrupting her thoughts with words that tumbled over themselves like white water. "I know we've never been, well, intimate before. We haven't even talked about this sort of thing. But I've found myself in love. Admiring you. Seeing how beautiful you are. I'm convinced you could fall in love with me, too. You're serious, intelligent, sensitive, and well, did I tell you you were beautiful? I'm saying a lot, I know. So stop me if I've gone too far...."

So that was it. He loved her, he wanted to marry her. She smiled up at him, and that simple encouragement made him swiftly rise from his seat and hold out his arms to her. Without knowing it, she stood up to respond to him.

"My love, I will do everything to make you happy," he said, as his powerful arms enveloped her. It was not until he pulled away from her to pull a handkerchief from his pocket that she realized she was crying. It was so simple— the man of her dreams must have been right next to her all along. Suddenly the future didn't seem so frightening, so purposeless. The one thing that had scared her, the sense of not having a home, had been destroyed. Home would be wherever Robert took her—wherever he went.

"Don't tell me your answer now," Robert was saying. "I've gotten everything so out of order. I've been shut up in an ivory tower so long I've forgotten I'm supposed to ask you out on a date first. And me, an anthropologist—I don't even follow the courtship rituals of my own culture."

"What if I told you my answer was yes?"

"To getting married?"

She nodded, her eyes brimming with tears of happiness.

"I'd say we better wait to have our first date until after we get married," he answered. His face, which had been tense and nervous, broke into a relaxed grin. It took several seconds before Casey realized he was making a joke, his first in her presence.

She smiled up at him.

"We could get married today and have our first date tonight," Robert continued.

"Yeah, but what are we going to do for a second date?" Casey asked, still stunned by the events of the past ten minutes.

They didn't get married that day. Or even the next. They had to wait a month to get married, between the mandatory blood test and Casey studying for finals.

But when they did get married there was a lot of talk at the school. There were rumors that Casey had some sort of sexual hold on Robert. Men she had never given the time of day to started claiming that they had gone out with the "ice princess" and when she got into bed she was a tiger.

Robert's colleagues ostracized him, faculty wives being terribly unsympathetic about liaisons with students. Only Harry Kramer, chairman of the department, toasted the newlyweds, taking them to dinner one night to celebrate their wedding. Robert didn't seem to notice the slights and insults, but Casey did—and she felt even more lonely than before she was married.

Which seemed silly, because if she was in love, wasn't she supposed to not feel that gut-wrenching loneliness?

She buried her self-doubts in a pile of work, desperately trying to match her husband's pace—helping him grade the hundreds of exams, reading research abstracts and packing for the trek.

It was then that she realized her own ambition and potential for hard work. Paradoxically, her marriage to Robert had convinced her that her love for anthropology wasn't simply a devotion to the taciturn genius. She began to harbor what she knew were silly fantasies of professional success of her own, apart from Robert, out from under his shadow.

That June, she followed Robert to Alaska, moving into the small hotel his friend Skip owned, using the hotel as a base camp between expeditions to Athabascan settlements. Actually, hotel was something of a misnomer—there were seldom any overnight guests. Sometimes a tour group stopped in, or a crowd of trappers looking for a warm bath and a good night's sleep while on the road, some natives, some pipeline workers. But most of the time, Skip, Robert and Casey had free run of the place. It was like being one of the three musketeers for Casey; she felt as though something was settled in her life, something resolved.

She had found that sense of belonging she had longed for. She was excited that fall—not only did she have someplace to go for Thanksgiving and Christmas, but that place was truly home. Even now, she had to smile at the memory of that holiday season. Baking cookies with Skip, ordering presents from one of the shops at Fort Yukon, decorating the cabin.

Even Robert seemed more relaxed, and at night, when she would whisper that she loved him before they fell asleep, he would answer that he loved her, too.

If only life could have remained that way forever.

Her reverie was interrupted by a loud, insistent pounding on the door of the cabin. Casey came back to the present. There was no Robert, she remembered, feeling the emptiness of the last year.

There was no Robert coming home tonight.

Skip jumped up and set his coffee cup down on the mantel.

"That must be your Mr. Brodie," he said, and walked to the door.

Joseph stirred at her feet, waking slowly, without crying. She smiled at him as he opened his eyes and focused on her face. He smiled at her in a broad, two-tooth grin that suffused his face with joy.

"Hello, precious," she whispered. She leaned down and picked him up, sitting him on her lap.

Skip yanked open the front door, and a gust of wind shot through the room. The few papers that Casey had left on the bar—notes for the lecture on her fieldwork, which she would give at the university—fluttered to the floor. Casey felt the chilly draft shoot clear through to her bones and she clutched her son more tightly. She looked to the doorway and saw only a large, dark shadow blocking out the sunlit sky beyond the open door.

Chapter Three

"Get on in here, you're letting the heat escape," Skip said, waving the dark shadow into the light of the fireplace and slamming shut the door. "What do you think this is—the Caribbean?"

Casey stared up at him, at Leon Brodie, and was stunned that he was everything that she had remembered: eyes that reflected an emerald light from the fire, hair the color of dark ravens and a muscular sense that spoke volumes about his strength and vigor. The reality of him was so much like her memory—a memory she had returned to, if she was honest, nearly every day since Joseph's birth—and it was as if he had never been away.

Instantly she felt guilty, an emotion that had plagued her since their first meeting. How could she hold the picture of this flyboy, a man with whom she had only spent a few hours—an emotion-packed few hours, she admitted—while her memory of Robert faded more every day? She could only picture her dead husband if she sat quietly and concentrated, pushing away the insistent demands of the day and the awakening suspicion that something had been terribly wrong with her marriage, something that clearly must have been her fault.

Leon pulled his jacket off to reveal broad, muscular shoulders, captive beneath a bright red flannel shirt and thermal underwear. He and Casey stared at each other silently, grimly—each somehow dreaded and, yet, was attracted to the other.

"You want a cup of coffee, or something stronger?" Skip asked gruffly, breaking the mood.

"Coffee will be fine," Leon replied, his eyes drifting from Casey only to look at Joseph, who silently sucked on his thumb. "He's gotten a lot bigger."

Casey nodded at the understatement.

Leon pushed a hunk of the wavy, blue-black hair away from his eyes and sat in the wing chair across the rug from Casey. She touched her hand to the base of her neck, unconsciously stemming an involuntary shift in the rhythm of her heart.

There were plenty of men in Alaska, available men who would be thrilled to have a twenty-five-year-old woman, even with her six-month-old baby. Casey had been fending off suitors since before the ground had settled on Robert's grave. Trappers, pilots, geologists from the oil companies—Casey felt the pressure, particularly when an astute wooer would transfer his attentions to Joseph in the hope that such a move would melt her heart. But, of course, she kept to herself, shaking off men like dust. With Leon not even expressing any interest yet, why was she concerned about whether he would challenge her solitude?

"Name's Leon Brodie, you might remember me, ma'am." Leon leaned back in his chair and rolled up his sleeves, all without taking his eyes from her. "I didn't recognize you for a moment, having never seen you when you aren't pregnant."

Casey nodded in reply, biting her tongue. He had brought a funny smell into the room, some masculine mix of gasoline and hard sweat. It wasn't unpleasant, but it was so... dangerous, posing a threat to the hard-won stability of her life after Robert's death.

"She does look pretty different, about twenty pounds lighter," Skip agreed and handed Leon a cup of coffee. He retrieved his own from the mantel and positioned himself next to Casey. "You and your friend Dodge did us a mighty big favor when Joseph was born, though Dodge was a little miffed when Casey named her baby Joseph and saved only the middle name for him. He thinks you can't have too many babies named Calvin or Dodge."

The three chuckled, Skip's comment easily breaking the tension.

"I think you two are in a somewhat different relationship now—Casey Stevens is your boss," Skip continued.

Leon's eyes betrayed a hint of surprise.

"When Calvin asked me to do him a favor and pick up a load here, I guess I had just assumed it was for you, Skip," he said, his southern drawl pleasantly strong. "I don't work for Calvin, but he didn't have a pilot out in this neck of the woods."

"I'm going to leave the state for good. I came here to work with my husband," Casey explained, conscious that she was using Robert to push this flyboy away. "I've lost my husband, so I'm going Outside," she finished.

"I'm sorry to hear that," he said. "About your husband, that is. I'm sure you'll be happy Outside."

Skip shifted his weight from one leg to another. The prospect of Casey and Joseph leaving had always caused him to fidget. It was a sore point between him and Casey.

Couldn't he understand? Casey asked herself, sneaking a glance at him. Couldn't he understand that she needed to go? She would miss him, Joseph would miss him. Casey bit her lip, determined not to reopen the discussion with him. It always ended badly, perhaps because they were so close. The last time they had argued about it had been yesterday, and Skip had spent the evening with tightly pursed lips and a sour expression.

One of the fireplace's three glowing red Sitka spruce logs shifted and dropped, sending a gray cloud of ash into the living room.

"I think it's strained peaches time for Mr. Joseph," Skip said with artificial brightness, pulling Joseph from Casey's arms before she could protest. "I'll be in the kitchen while you two friends get reacquainted."

Good old Skip, Casey thought, leaving me with the flyboy when I don't have the slightest idea of how to start a conversation with him. Skip was good with people, Casey protested silently, and she was too shy. She stared out past the darkness of the living room to the solitary window.

She was reminded of her real problem. The plane. The small plane. What could she do? Try to make other arrangements? Maybe he could fly her and Joseph and the exhibit pieces in two trips to Anchorage. Then she could take a commercial flight to Chicago, sending the exhibit pieces by courier. It sounded expensive. Harry, still chairman of the anthropology department, had already told her that he couldn't get the university to forward the honorarium before the lecture, but he had offered to loan her some money himself. She had refused, determined not to take more from him than was necessary. He had already done so much to make the exhibit possible.

"It's an awful hard load you carry, raising a baby out here in the middle of nowhere. Nearest town is what—ten, twenty miles away?" Leon's sympathetic voice, as soft and warm as butter, startled her so much she nearly spilled her coffee.

"Twenty—at least, that's one of the settlements. Fort Yukon is a hundred miles away. That's where we get our supplies."

"Still, it's got to be hard. I'm a man and not even tied down anywhere, and sometimes even I find it a little rough here in Alaska."

"Well, luckily, I'm getting out of here permanently," she said abruptly. Instantly she was ashamed by her horrid tone and unable to stop herself from continuing, she blurted out, "I hate this place."

He leaned back and crossed his legs, his faint smile dying. The warmth in his eyes went out, leaving a cold, sea-green glint. Casey shifted in her chair, suddenly uneasy. Every word she had spoken seemed to push him away, marking out a territory and firmly declaring herself off-limits. The friendly, open manner he'd had when he entered the cabin dissolved. She couldn't blame him.

"Well, maybe we should talk about something else. Let's stick with business, and business means money." His mouth tightened. "I'll be charging you the fee you agreed to with Calvin. I don't know how he handles money, but I ask for half up front and half when I get you where you're going."

"I don't have the money yet," Casey admitted. "But I can pay after my lecture. See, when I talked to Calvin, I didn't know that the university wouldn't pay me until—"

"Half up front and half when the job is done," he interrupted.

Casey felt a red flush of anger cover her face, reaching to the roots of her hair. He had put her on the defensive. And he had no right to. After all, he was the one with the wrong plane.

"I started to tell you, the university will reimburse me after the exhibit is—"

"I can't tell you how many times somebody's stiffed me, and—"

Casey's temper boiled over, although a needling voice in the back of her head insisted that she wasn't angry at Leon over a plane so much as over a memory, over a dead man, over a lifetime of insecurities that he threatened.

"You can't possibly think you'll transport me, my baby and the artifacts in that plane out there!"

"Whoa there, lady, nobody told me about a baby. I'm not interested in transporting any crying babies in my plane. And as for the artifacts, what could you possibly have? A couple of scrimshaw carvings?"

"There's baskets and moose hide with beading and some of their musical instruments—drums, mostly. I'm going to need help getting to some of the settlements to pick things up that I can't get to in the Land Rover and then, since it's obvious you can't get me to Chicago, I'll have to make other arrangements—once you get me to Anchorage."

"Most shuttle services would only do the same."

"But Calvin said you would get me all the way to Chicago."

He shrugged, unwilling to commit himself to agreeing with her.

What had Calvin been thinking of? they thought simultaneously, each determined to have a little talk with him at the earliest possible moment.

For an instant, Casey thought he would leave, just get up out of his chair and leave her to find another pilot. But much as she hated him at this moment, for making things even more difficult than they had been, she couldn't send him away.

She needed transport to Chicago. And if he couldn't get her there, then at least to Calvin's headquarters in Anchorage. Once she was in Anchorage she could make other arrangements.

Their eyes met in a standoff. He turned his head first, letting her determined stare—no, glare—chasten him. They sipped their coffee silently, as if they were an old married couple angry at each other.

Thankfully, Skip poked his head out the kitchen door.

"Can you get in here, Casey?" he asked. "This boy of yours thinks peaches are meant to be sprayed out of your mouth instead of eaten."

Casey jumped up and ran to the brightly lit kitchen. What a sight! Her little Joseph sat in his high chair, everything—his face, his hair, his ears—covered with pale orange streaks. He smiled up at her, proudly showing off his two new bottom teeth. Then, brandishing the spoon he must have wrestled from Skip's hand, he scrunched his face and spit out a new stream of fruit, beating his spoon on the high-chair table.

"I think I liked it better when he was eating food that was white, like the rice and the tapioca pudding," Skip said, barely controlling his laughter. "It seemed to blend in with everything better."

Joseph let out an ecstatic yelp as Casey took the dish towel from Skip. Clearly Mommy was going to help him eat.

"Isn't that beef stew I smell?" she asked. Her mouth ached from the sudden rush of saliva. Had she forgotten lunch? How long had it been since breakfast?

"Yeah, I'm trying a new recipe—deer, bay leaf, some vegetables, and my secret ingredient."

"Sherry," Casey guessed, breathing in the sweet, spicy steam that had overtaken the kitchen. "Sherry and honey."

"Okay, not so secret," Skip countered.

"You think you have enough to give me a little supper?" Leon asked, brushing past her—after a moment in which he fleetingly rested his strong hands on her shoulders.

"Grab a bowl from the cupboard over the sink," Skip ordered Leon. In Alaska, there wasn't a single kitchen that wouldn't be hospitable to others and Skip's was no exception. "Casey, stop staring off into space like a teenager and start feeding your boy. I'll get your dinner put down. Want some corn bread with your stew?"

"Please." Casey nodded and sat at the table. She pulled the high chair in front of her. Within minutes, Skip and Leon had put down hot buttered slices of bread, bowls of stew and three glasses of beer.

"You sure I should have a beer?" Casey asked Skip, eyeing the frothy golden liquid.

"It's a celebration," Skip exclaimed, pushing the glass into her hand. He nudged Leon. "She's not very good at holding her liquor. Actually, she's a lot of fun when she's not very good at holding her liquor. Did you know she once sang the entire score, I think they call it libretto, of some danged opera to a bunch of trappers from—"

"Skip!"

Skip leaned back and shrugged.

"All right, Casey, I won't say anything. But I think you ought to join in a toast to our friend Leon Brodie."

Casey hurriedly shoved a spoonful of stew into her mouth between spoonfuls of peaches given to her son. She tried to ignore Skip's magnanimous toast to the pilot. He never passed up the opportunity for an impromptu holiday. He knew the birthdays of every president, vice president and Alaskan governor, territorial and state, in case he ran out of more personal causes for celebration.

When Skip was done singing the praises of Leon, of pilots, of young men and of anyone else he could think of, she joined the men's hurrahs and took a tentative sip of her beer, all the while juggling the insistent demands of both her growling stomach and her baby boy.

"Why don't you let me take a spin at it?" Leon asked, taking Joseph's tiny spoon from her hand. "Get yourself fed."

Casey hesitated for a moment, but the gnawing at her stomach won out. She had to admit she was hungry. She passed the baby spoon and the bowl of peaches to Leon, and took a fast gulp of her beer. He pushed his chair so that he sat on the other side of Joseph.

"Here you go, boy."

Joseph looked down at the food and then up at Leon.

"No, not like that—too full a spoon and you'll drop more than you'll get in his mouth." Casey said between mouthfuls of stew.

"Okay, okay." Leon tried again, but, with a pixieish smile, Joseph foiled him. "Hey, he won't open his mouth!"

"Just leave the spoon under his nose, eventually he'll open up. He's just playing with you."

She continued to eat, shoving corn bread and stew into her mouth while she and Skip watched Leon's efforts.

"He won't keep his head still."

"Well, follow his mouth," Skip advised.

After trailing the recalcitrant Joseph with the spoon without success, Leon threw down the baby spoon.

"I give up," he said, good-naturedly. "I guess baby feeding isn't my best sport."

Casey shrugged. The beer was having its effect—she felt a tad friendlier toward him. And somehow less frightened of his presence. She picked up the spoon.

"Baby feeding doesn't look like something you're called upon all that often to do."

"Never will be."

Casey looked up at him, distracted from her attempt to get Joseph to open his mouth.

"Never?"

"Never," Leon said, with finality. "I don't want to ever get tied down with a woman, much less a baby. If you ask me, women are just looking for men to fix their lives for them and they take away a man's freedom—the things that make getting up in the morning worth it. I just don't aim to do that for any woman."

Casey rose in her seat, ready to defend every member of her sex, and in particular, herself—because it was hard not to think of his words as a personal attack.

"You think love is just a plot by women to take away your right to go off and do the things men do—the stupid poker games and reading *Playboy* and getting to drink milk out of the carton?"

"Well, it's certainly what marriage is, isn't it?" Leon asked.

Skip, who had been quiet, put his spoon in his empty bowl and took a final swig of beer.

"Now, children," he said, and he took Joseph's spoon from Casey. "I will take care of the baby while you get your dinner in your gullet. I think the battle of the sexes for this evening is a draw. Leon, you'll be taking one of the guest rooms for this evening. It's not much, but there's not another hotel, motel, or even a house for at least six or seven miles, maybe more.''

Casey looked up at Leon, into those laughing eyes. He smiled with a damnably superior air, as if it were some sort of mark of honor not to ever be "tied down." As if she'd want to do the tying.

Well, Casey thought triumphantly, *he's just enough of an ass that I don't have to take him the slightest bit seriously.*

The three passed the rest of the meal in silence. Skip gave Joseph a teething cookie and retired to the living room, where he proceeded to play a few of his ragtime favorites. Uncomfortably aware of her nearness to Leon, Casey hurriedly finished the last of her beer and picked up Joseph. Leon followed her into the living room.

"Why don't you try a spin around the floor together?" Skip called out, not missing a note in the complex and spritely tune he was playing. Casey turned and looked at Leon. Dance with him? How utterly ridiculous.

And how strangely alluring.

She shook her head.

"Oh, come on!" Skip shouted and played all the more loudly.

"Well?" Leon asked. "What do you think?"

Casey imagined being pulled into his arms. She imagined him holding her so tightly she had to arch her back so she wouldn't crush her face into his chest. She imagined looking into his eyes, certain he was going to kiss her, right there, as they danced around the living-room floor—his lips, full and hard, ready to crush her own.

"I would be honored to have this dance," Leon said as courtly as a prince, and pulled Joseph from her arms.

Utterly baffled, she watched as her son whirled and turned and waltzed along the living-room floor in Leon's capable arms. For a brief instant, she was perversely jealous and felt an awkward aloneness—a left-outness. But, watching her giggling, delighted boy in the arms of a mock-serious suitor, the maternal joy in Joseph's happiness won out and she sank into the nearest chair with a contented sigh. The music grew louder and louder, the shrieks of her ecstatic son matching Skip's playing note for note.

She hadn't been this happy since...

The smile died on her lips and her eyes dropped guiltily to watch the expiring fire. When the music stopped and Leon stood before her with an out-of-breath infant, it was easy to see that the gay mood had been broken. She stood up, and taking Joseph from Leon's arms, buried her head briefly in her baby's shoulders, smelling the fresh-breadlike scent of his hair. With a curt good-night, she fled upstairs.

Leon stared after her, baffled and annoyed.

"What got her goat?" he asked Skip.

Skip closed the lid on the piano keys.

"When she lost her husband, she thought she lost her life," he said, and shuffled to the bar. "She really depended on him."

"A woman like that doesn't belong around here," Leon countered, accepting a beer. "Maybe she belongs Outside, where she can find some guy to take care of her."

"That's what she thinks, too," Skip said ruefully.

When Skip came upstairs, he found her dozing on the rocking chair in Joseph's room, the sleeping baby lying on her lap. Skip woke her and gently pulled at Joseph. The sleeping baby's eyes briefly opened, startled at the interruption.

"Come on, pardner, time to go to bed and chase all the little sheep," he said, laying Joseph in his crib and placing a comforting hand on the baby's back until he settled back into sleep.

"What time is it?" Casey asked wearily. How could it be that one minute she was singing to Joseph and the next minute she was watching him being put in his crib?

"It's only ten," Skip said. "Your Mr. Brodie is already off to sleep, and I'd suggest you do the same. You have a lot of work tomorrow."

She stood up and walked to the door. Boy, that beer had made her head feel as if a jackhammer was drilling through it—then she processed Skip's words.

"By the way, Skip, he's not *my* Mr. Brodie."

As he leaned over Joseph, arranging the blankets, she could barely see his cheeks broaden in a smile.

"Don't be so hard on me," Skip said. "I only thought you being a woman alone that you might think the guy is attractive. My handsome self being a mite too old for you, you might be willing to settle for second best."

He stood up, after placing a gentle kiss on Joseph's cheek.

"If I can find a man around these parts for you to hitch up with, then you'll stick around," he continued, ignoring her protest. "And I'll get to see my only chance at a grandson grow up. You can hardly blame an old man for trying."

"You're laying it on a little thick," Casey teased, her easy tone belying the tension that came between them with increasing frequency. "I can't spend the rest of my life here. I hate Alaska," she finished, with a little more stridency than she intended. "It's too lonely out here."

"You like it fine. You hate crowds, you can't stand noisy people, and you like to fish too much to live in Chicago. I'm telling you, Casey, you're going to miss me and the whole bloody state of Alaska."

"Maybe so," Casey said quietly. "But how about if for tonight, I just get some sleep."

Skip nodded and put a comforting arm around her.

"I shouldn't bother you about it," he said as they left the bedroom. "I guess being a confirmed old bachelor, I'm starting to realize Joseph and you are the most important people in my life."

They hugged and Casey fought the impulse to reassure him that she would change her plans, stay in Alaska, never leave him.

Instead she whispered good-night and went into her room.

Later, as she pulled her down blanket around her shoulders, on the solitary bed she had once shared with Robert, she felt the familiar twins: panic and loneliness.

Robert, she silently prayed, I miss you so much.

And, feeling it was heresy, she quelled her doubts: the doubts about her marriage, about Robert, about herself.

Downstairs, in one of the guest rooms, Leon Brodie sat in bed, staring out the window at the ridge of white-capped mountains.

The woman irritated him in a way he couldn't put his finger on. He had remembered every detail about her, having thought of her frequently at odd moments during the past six months. He loved the auburn hair that sparkled in the light of the fire. Those eyes that gave her away so easily when she was angry. The skin, so pale, he imagined tracing his finger along the tiny part of her collarbone that had been exposed beneath her shirt and following the trail of skin down her chest, touching the soft breasts, the warm rounded belly... Leon pulled off his shirt.

It suddenly seemed hot in the room.

That woman, with the baby resting on her lap, was so domestic. It frightened him the way he had instantly thought, "This is the kind of life I would like, coming home to my woman with my baby on her lap."

Maybe that was what was so irritating about her. It was how she made him think about a kind of life he had long ago rejected. He had seen the way women looked at him. He knew he was attractive, but not handsome. He wasn't perfect-featured enough for handsome—not after his nose had been broken years ago in a bar fight. Some women were scared off when they realized he wasn't rich. His father had left him some money, but no one knew about it. Some women were scared off when they realized he wasn't going to make a commitment. Some women hung in there a while, hoping that although he said he wasn't interested in settling down, he'd change his mind. But he never did.

Nothing had ever mattered to him except flying. His mother had run off with another man when Leon was two, and after that it had just been him and his dad. And his dad's favorite pastime, aside from buying and selling real estate in the small Alabama town he had always called home, was hopping into a plane and seeing the country from a mile up in the air. And of course, Leon went along.

He had gotten his pilot's license when he was fourteen, the youngest age you could, and he'd been flying without a license in his father's two-seater for a year before that. When his father had died, in Leon's junior year at college, he left Leon the two-seater and a crumbling real-estate empire. By the time the debts were settled, there were only a few thousand dollars left. Leon put it in the bank, determined to "forget" the money until he really needed it. He dropped out of college, took the plane out of the hangar and set off for the rest of his life.

There was no doubt that he was a good pilot, and could make enough to satisfy his needs. Alaska had been particularly good to him; the state was so dependent on the itinerant pilots who ferry everything and everyone. And the solitary life-style that many Alaskans live was perfect for him—and the years had quickly passed.

That was what had been bugging him—he was starting to feel his age. When he had been in college, and had spent more time taking the girls up in his plane than studying, it had felt like the skies opened up to him with a promise of a future that stretched out forever. Now, at thirty-five, *forever* seemed a little more tiring than he had bargained for.

He pulled out an envelope from inside the shirt that he had carelessly dropped on the floor. He opened it and read the letter for what had to be the hundredth time.

It was from Calvin Dodge, and although the two men talked nearly every week, the letter was something much more formal and serious than anything they had ever discussed. Calvin had opened a commuter airline in Alaska— transporting traders and tourists in six-seaters, twin-engines and prop planes up and down the state—and he was offering Leon a chance to buy in . . . to fly and to own part of the business. Calvin must have known that Leon was too proud simply to be an employee.

In the recent months, Calvin had been calling upon Leon for more and more "favor" flights, transporting furs and supplies and people around the state when Calvin couldn't find a pilot of his own. And the offer to buy into the business was looking more and more like an inevitable rather than a far-off possibility.

It's a compromise, Leon thought to himself—able to fly but tied down. So far, he didn't see any payoff to being tied down—to not being able to take off into the skies and follow the sun or the stars without an agenda.

Leon carefully folded the letter back into its envelope. One job at a time, he thought. These transport jobs were letting him put a little money aside and see a little more of the country, even if he had to work with a woman like Casey Stevens.

He'd finish this one for Calvin, even though he thought it was pretty damn strange that Calvin had not told him who he'd be working for. Maybe he'd join Calvin's company, but only after he gave him a piece of his mind about working for Casey Stevens.

Chapter Four

Casey awakened as she always did: startled by the sound of Joseph's crying. She rolled over and looked at the clock by her bed. Six-thirty, an average night's sleep for her baby. Struggling to stand, she pulled on the dark blue flannel robe that lay at the foot of the bed. She felt as if something was missing, and for just a moment, stood in the dark bedroom wondering what she had been expecting when she awoke.

It was like having a dream and forgetting it. She knew there was something she had been thinking of, expecting, anticipating, but whatever it was was just outside of her reach.

Joseph gave another yelp, and she abandoned her thoughts. When she opened the bedroom door, she halted and reflexively clutched the doorjamb, her heart seeming to leap toward her throat.

In her groggy, half-awake state, she saw a shadowy figure at the end of the hall. Taller and more muscular than

Skip. Instantly mindful of her son in the next room, she planted her feet squarely in line with her shoulders.

"Who's there?" she demanded, with as much conviction as she could muster.

"It's Leon," the figure said, coming into the circle of light from the lamp over Casey's door. "What's all the commotion?"

Casey released the breath she had been holding.

The man had no right to scare her like that!

Her irritation rose as her eyes focused on his bare chest...the sharply defined upper arms...the line of hair that suggestively drew her eyes down to the zipper of his jeans. Those jeans were so tight that a woman would have to be comatose not to notice the suggestive bulge of his thigh muscles.

Wide-awake, she launched an offensive.

"It's a baby. Haven't you ever heard one?"

She rushed down the hallway to Joseph's room. Joseph stood at the crib bars, arms outstretched, face wet with frantic tears. When he saw her, he wiped his nose with his fist and reached out for his mommy.

She switched on the light and pulled Joseph into her arms. She could feel Leon standing in the doorway, watching her, and she felt as if his stare was burning a hole in her back. She whispered soothing words into Joseph's ears, and he clutched her, shoving his head into the soft corner made by her neck and shoulders, padded by the soft flannel of her robe.

"When he was first born, he got up at least twice a night," Casey said, hoping to fill the quiet morning air with conversation. Why did Leon make her so uncomfortable? "When he started sleeping through the night at three months, I was still waking up in the middle of the night, coming into his room to look at him—to make sure he was still breathing. Every mother does that, I'm sure. Now I sleep through the night, but I know he wakes up about a half hour before he cries. He plays with his feet or his bear, and then he remembers that he wants me."

She turned around to face him. Leon slouched against the door, staring her up and down with lazy, half-closed eyes. When her gaze met his, she realized what she had thought was missing when she woke up. She had somehow thought she should wake up sleeping next to this stranger. His arms entwined with hers, that tangle of chest hair pressed against her back, that robustly masculine scent on her sheets.

She bristled, and pressed her face against her baby's head to shut out the onslaught of emotions. Was she being disloyal to Robert with these utterly involuntary feelings?

It wasn't the idea of going out with another man, or even marrying. She knew enough to realize that her life had to go on, someday, without Robert. No, the disloyalty to Robert was even worse—she was feeling decidedly hot, decidedly indecent, sexual feelings for this nearly total stranger, feelings that she had despaired of ever feeling for Robert.

She looked up at him, eyes narrowing with an irrational hostility directed at a man who threatened the grim, but secure, future she had carved out for herself, a man who threatened the very fabric of her life.

"Well, I guess I better leave you guys alone," Leon said, his hesitant tone a reflection of his confusion about her sudden coldness. "I just heard the noise and thought something was wrong."

She stared silently at him and he walked away without another word. When she could no longer hear his footsteps, she kissed Joseph's forehead, drawing comfort from her baby's simple joy in her touch.

Guilty! Guilty! Guilty! her conscience screamed.

But why shouldn't I have a chance to think about other men? she asked silently.

Think of all Robert did for you, the voice reminded.

"What do you say we go get some breakfast, Joseph?" she whispered, determined to distract herself from destructive thinking.

Many mornings, she would go back to bed, letting Joseph rest beside her, cuddling and chattering. But this morning, she wanted the day to start early—Leon's imprint was already on her bed.

She hastily changed into jeans and a sweater and took Joseph downstairs to the kitchen. Skip was there, making coffee and firing up the stove for eggs and bacon.

"I wasn't expecting you for another half hour or so," he said, blowing a kiss to Joseph.

"I want to get an early start," Casey lied. "Where's Leon?"

"He went back to his room, said he wanted to sleep another hour. You have to feel sorry for a man who doesn't even know what a baby's crying sounds like." He took Joseph from her arms and settled him into his high chair.

"Feeling sorry for him wasn't quite what I was thinking of."

She picked out a can of baby food from the cabinet. She held up her choice, bananas in tapioca, for Joseph to see. He shrieked with delight, clapping his hands together. She sat down in a chair in front of him and Skip handed her Joseph's baby spoon and his bowl.

"You forgot these," he said.

"Sorry. I'm a little tired."

He fixed her a cup of coffee and put it on the table, far enough away from Joseph so that there was no chance of an accident.

"What's on the agenda today?" he asked.

"I'm going to have Leon take me up to the village to pick up the remaining baskets."

"That should be all you need for the exhibit?"

Casey nodded.

Skip sat across from her with his plate of eggs.

"You want me to finish feeding Joseph, give you a chance to eat your own?" Skip asked, shoveling a forkful of scrambled eggs into his mouth.

Casey shook her head.

"I don't get much chance to do all the things that a mother does," she said. "You do so much for him."

"If he had a father, that father would feed him when you weren't around, he would change a few diapers, and later on he'd teach him how to play catch."

"But he doesn't have a father."

"He could have one if you tried. There are a lot of men around these parts who wouldn't object to having a wife like you."

There it was again—Skip's anger about her leaving. He wanted her to stay, wanted her to build her life here, without Robert. But she had to go, even if it meant leaving him behind. She wanted to return to the university, to the safety that a life of the mind, a life devoted to study, offered.

"I'm not in the market for a husband," Casey said, not daring to let her eyes meet Skip's. "Well, at least not for the kind of men I meet around here." Seeing his pout, she tried some levity. "Sorry, I didn't mean you, Skip. If they were all like you, darling..."

Joseph protested his mother's momentary lapse in attention and Casey offered him another spoonful of his breakfast.

"Don't you ever wonder why you chose Robert as a husband?" Skip asked.

The question took Casey by surprise. She stared at Skip for several seconds, her marine-blue eyes shining with anger. What could Skip know about Robert and her? Sure, the two men had been friends, but she had always sensed she was closer to Skip than Robert ever was.

Was she wrong? Were there secrets about Robert that even she didn't know?

"What kind of question is that?" she asked at last.

Skip's eyes softened with love for her.

"Robert told me he knew that you married him more out of your insecurity about the future than out of any great love," he said. When Casey started to rise from her seat with indignation, he put a hand on her shoulder. "You idolized him as a teacher, thought he was a god, admired his mind—but all that isn't really love."

Casey looked away, her blue eyes blazing with a fire as icy cold as the diamond engagement ring she still wore on her right hand as a companion to her wedding band.

"Love is when he walks into the room and the lights seem brighter because of it," Skip said. "Love is when you can't stand to eat when he's away, and food never tastes better than when he's with you. Love is when you can't even think about another man, no matter how good-looking. Love is when you can't hold anything back."

"I've heard just about enough!" Casey stared at Skip, her brutal eyes commanding him.

"Well, did you love him that way?"

Casey gaped at him for a minute. What right did he have to ask questions like that? Uncomfortable questions.

"I don't think I need to answer that," Casey said with as much dignity as she possessed.

Skip stood up.

"You're right. You don't have to answer," he said softly. He sauntered over to the sink with forced casualness. "But how about one other question, Casey? Do you think he loved you that way?"

Casey slumped in her seat, feeling drained. Her head was spinning, but she took a few deep breaths, struggling to regain her composure. Joseph slapped his hands on the high-chair tray and she smiled absently at him.

"By the way, he knew you were pregnant when he went out." Skip didn't have to say that he meant the last day that Robert was alive. "And it made him happy. Somehow he knew that you would be a very good mother. He was my friend, and I don't mean to be disloyal, but he could never love a woman the way you need to be loved."

A raging flame, fueled by guilt and longing, seared through her, and for a moment, she thought she would blow up at Skip—unleasing the frustrations and disappointments of the last year. Instead she took a deep, cooling breath and counted to ten.

"I've got to get that flyboy ready to go," she said, turning away. "We've got a lot of work."

She picked up Joseph from his high chair and bolted for the door to the living room. She wanted to cry out, to deny everything Skip had said and implied, but how could she when she was guilty as charged? She had loved Robert—in her own fashion. And she had never lied to him, well, except for one lie—the lie that she had told again and again, but only because the truth, a sexual truth, was beyond her grasp.

And what did Skip mean, that Robert couldn't love her the way she needed to be loved? A doubt, something she had denied for so long, threatened to erupt full-blown into her consciousness—a doubt about his warmth, a doubt about the love he professed to have for her, a doubt about the happiness she would have enjoyed had he lived.

"Casey," Skip said quietly, startling her by his entry into the living room.

"What?"

"He loved you very much, but don't ever confuse what he felt for you with something else."

And he turned back into the kitchen before she could ask him what that something else was.

Leon pulled the throttle up, driving the plane's nose up into the sparkling sun. Reveling in the unbridled horizon of cloud and sky, he nearly forgot about the woman beside him. He had often been with people who were afraid of flying—white-knuckle fliers, they were called.

But Casey was the worst. She hadn't said a word to him since they had taken off and her hands never moved, clenched together in two, tiny white fists on her lap.

And her mouth, a mouth that he had admired the evening before for its swollen rosiness, was now rigidly pursed.

How could any Alaskan afford to be so scared of flying? he wondered. The state being so large, nearly a fifth of the size of the entire rest of the United States, air travel was the only way to get around.

"This is a great plane, originally built in the late forties," he explained to Casey. Damn, she made him so nervous that he was defending his own plane!

"I just hope she's in good condition," Casey said in a stilted voice, staring grimly out her passenger-side window at the snow-fringed mountain ridge. Only six hundred feet in the air, they were still below the few clouds that marred the otherwise jarringly sunny sky.

They flew silently over the ridge, onto a plain dotted with green pine and white and blue spruce. Caribou herds galloped through the trees, startled by the noise of the airplane. Leon felt the familiar peacefulness wash over him. He never felt completely comfortable unless he was in the air.

Now, of course, he was home, if the dome of the sky surrounding the whole of Alaska could be considered a single house.

They had left as soon as Leon had bolted down a breakfast of salmon steak and eggs. Concerned about a takeoff on ice and snow, he had used a wet trail of green muskegon as a runway.

"I've been flying ever since I was a kid," he explained to her, thinking that if he interested her in conversation, she would calm down. "My father was in the air force, before he started a real-estate business in Alabama. Had a little farm—used the fields more for runways than for tobacco. Got my pilot's license when I was fourteen. When I was in college, all I did was fly."

She looked at him with surprise.

"You went to college?"

"Yeah, the local junior college. I didn't finish. Spent too much time flying, chasing girls and playing softball."

She turned back away, uninterested again.

"Did you go to college?" Leon asked. She was a tough customer—hardest woman he had ever talked to. And the questions about his education rankled. It was hard not to miss how she looked down on him.

"University of Chicago."

"Is that where you met your husband?"

"He was my anthropology instructor."

"So, you were the teacher's pet."

Leon could have kicked himself, except for the fact that there wasn't any room in the plane to move.

She didn't look too pleased with him. In fact, she looked downright furious.

"Sorry," Leon said. "I guess that was uncalled for. I just meant to be friendly. I take it he was real smart."

"He was one of the most intelligent man I ever knew," Casey said quietly, the angry edge of her voice beginning to fade as she remembered Robert. "He knew more about the North American Indians than anyone. He wanted to work with the Athabascan because he felt they were the most neglected. I suppose he was also interested because he was part Athabascan, on his mother's side, or maybe his father's. I forget."

"The tribes have all been changing," Leon reminded her.

"Yeah, they have cable television at the village we're heading for. They get WGN-TV from Chicago."

"This far out?"

"Sure. And the teenagers listen to rock and roll, a lot of it heavy metal. These kids can't understand the music the elder women sing. And the youngsters dream of getting out of here and moving to the city. Problem is, they don't get the kind of education that prepares them for that sort of life."

Leon nodded and tried to concentrate on flying.

"Education must be very important to you," he said.

"More than anything," she said, warming up to the subject. "When I was young, I discovered that a good education was the only thing that could give someone a chance to make up for not having all the advantages."

A shadow of sadness washed over her face, and Leon had to stop himself from reaching out to touch her. There was pain there, real pain that he knew he could only guess at. Something terrible had happened to her, something that she had thought working hard at school would overcome.

He imagined her as a youngster, burying her head in a book to avoid feelings of hurt, taking a teacher's approval as a poor substitute for love.

He steadied the controls with his left hand and reached over to her with his right. She didn't resist the pressure of his touch, and let her fists be opened and her delicate fingers entwined with his.

"My dad left when I was young," she said slowly, her cloudy blue eyes staring resolutely at the horizon. "Mom died when I was eight. I heard it was cancer. But I think it was heartache."

"Where did you go then?" Leon asked softly.

"First my mom's parents took me in. Then they realized they were too old to take care of a kid—they wanted to enjoy their retirement, you know, travel a lot. So I was sent to my mom's sister."

"And?"

"Her husband didn't want another mouth to feed, not that I can blame him, they didn't have much money." She shrugged her shoulders. "You can guess the rest. I went through every relative on my mom's side, and then someone tracked down my dad's parents. By the time I went to college, I had lived with every relative I have, sometimes for as little as two weeks at a time."

Leon squeezed her hand.

"It's not that I was bad, or a troublemaker—quite the opposite. I mean, I really tried to be helpful, to be a good guest."

"But that's just the point—you were a guest."

"And a guest can always be asked to leave," she said ruefully. She smiled at him, a wistful smile that made a tenderness explode within him. "You really understand."

Leon nodded.

"Anyhow," Casey continued, "I guess I thought that if I was good in school, I could be somebody. You know, somebody special. I wasn't really talented in sports or music. And I'm not a great beauty."

"I beg to disagree, Mrs. Stevens," he said, turning his head to make eye contact. Damn, he thought, a man could drown in those eyes, those deep blue eyes. "I think you're beautiful."

Boy, did he feel silly once the words were out of his mouth! In all his experience with women, he had never said anything so uncalculated, so simple and unrehearsed. The words may have been the same as what he had said a hundred times to a hundred different women.

But there was a difference when he said them to Casey; the words were true.

"I'm not looking for compliments," she answered, the voice gentle enough so that he knew that she appreciated him. Leon felt unsteady, though he knew the plane was on course, calmly slicing through a windless sky.

She shook her head, as if trying to dislodge the intimacy she felt with him. She pulled her hand away, and whatever window of closeness there had been was shut.

"I don't like to talk about the past," she said.

Awkwardly silent, they flew over the mountain ridge and through the plains until he saw a small circle of cabins under a crest of pine trees. As in nearly every village he passed over these days, there was a satellite dish proudly displayed near the center.

"Is this it?"

"Yes," she answered, seemingly startled out of deep thought. "Just land on the field to your left and we'll load up."

"I should warn you," he said. "When kids see the plane, they go crazy, you know, wanting me to take them up, wanting to know if I've got candy or treats."

"You get a lot of that?"

He shrugged, thinking with a mixture of pride and awkwardness of the crowds of excited children who always approached his landings.

"Yeah, it's a common thing."

He landed the plane on the dirt-and-gravel patch that served as a runway. He wasn't surprised at the team of twenty or so children who ran out to greet them, racing from the village center with unzipped jackets flapping behind their backs. But he was utterly baffled when, as Casey flipped open her door and stood on the wing panel, the children crowded around her. No one seemed to notice Leon; it was the first time he had been upstaged in his own plane!

"Are you going to tell us stories? Did you bring us any treats?" several of the children shouted. "Do you want to play with us?"

"Yes, yes, and yes," Casey answered, climbing from the passenger seat of the plane, pulling out a tote bag loaded with candy bars and cookies, laughing at the children grabbing and pulling at her. "But I need to do some work."

"No, no, no!" the children screamed.

Alone as he watched Casey and the children marching toward the village, Leon jumped out to the ground. A single, dark-haired boy in a deerskin parka stared at him from behind the wing.

"What kind of candy you got?" he asked impassively.

"I think I have some lollipops," Leon answered, turning back to the plane.

"Nah, forget it," the youth said. "Casey's got better than that."

The boy fled, running to catch up with the other children.

The next few hours Leon spent tagging along behind Casey as she looked at the large and tiny baskets, the soapstone carvings, the beaded furs and moose hides. Each piece was reviewed with the elders who explained how the piece was made and the significance of each one. Casey made up index cards describing each piece's origins.

When they had loaded up the plane, Leon went to the propeller to get his plane ready for the return flight.

"Hold on," Casey said. "I promised the children a story."

She walked back to the settlement and, after loading the plane carefully to keep the weight even, Leon caught up with her. She was in one of the larger cabins, with the village children gathered around her.

She looked peaceful and happy, sitting by the fire with a small girl sitting on her lap. The light made the red in her hair sparkle like rubies. Leon felt a familiar stirring in his jeans, and the unfamiliar urge to pick her up into his arms and tenderly kiss the heart-shaped lips.

Maybe not tenderly.

Maybe devour them.

"Stop that," he said and was startled at the sound of his own voice. Luckily no one else in the room seemed to notice him talking to himself. Stop that, he repeated silently. Casey was, he knew, the type of woman he couldn't play games with; he couldn't just pick her up for a fling and then discard her. He was too aware of her, of her feelings, of the emotions he could stir up within her. He suspected that something in her marriage had been missing, something she would be too proud to admit. But he felt empathy for her, with the shortcomings that she had dealt with.

He felt torn, and wanted to pull away from her. If she became aware of him, aware of his desires, in the romantic sense, he would never get away—he would be trapped every bit as much as every married man he had ever pitied.

"Lucky thing she's not interested," he said, and started when one of the children at the back of the circle turned around to stare at him.

He had caught the look in Casey's eye when she had made clear the kind of educated man who interested her, and the dismissive tone of her voice when she had found out he had gone to a junior college and not to some fancy ivy league place.

She could look down on him all she wanted—he wasn't interested.

Leon mumbled something about being out at the plane to no one in particular, and walked out to the field. Good thing she's going to Chicago, he thought again. She belongs there.

Chapter Five

They passed the white-peaked mountains in a silence that matched the stillness of the land. Casey stared at the horizon, dipped in light of a late-afternoon pink- and baby-yellow sun. For reasons she couldn't yet fathom, her throat had choked and tears had sprung to her eyes as she had hugged each child in turn—it was another goodbye accompanied by the notion that it was a last one. So many times in her own childhood she had said goodbye to newly introduced girlfriends when a relative packed her off to another. Somewhere along the line the faces and names of friends had melted into a single, heartbreaking goodbye.

I don't want to say goodbye again, she admitted to herself, thinking of the open and trusting faces of her young Athabascan friends. She bit her lower lip until she thought she could taste the blood, determined to erase the doubt that accompanied her move to Chicago.

But the more immediate problem was controlling her fears; her palms were wet and her face burned. *Poor Rob-*

ert, she thought to herself, involuntarily drawn to think of what his last few hours had been like.

She felt unsettled, and she wondered if she weren't avoiding something when she obsessed about Robert's crash. Normally she wasn't given to dwelling on the problems or tragedies of the past—she worked hard to forget, to move on. She wanted to concentrate on the future—the lecture at the University of Chicago, getting a job at the university, finding someone to care for Joseph while she worked.

Casey watched Leon expertly and smoothly guide his craft over the mountains and plains. He tipped the wing just a shade, convincing Casey that they were soon to crash, and then he casually pointed out the window past her shoulder.

"There's the pipeline," he said, and she nodded at the sight of the slender steel path that stretched for forever and a herd of caribou that scattered, frightened by the noise of the engine. She looked at Leon as his eyes returned to observing the horizon in front of him.

Admit it, Casey thought, *you're avoiding letting yourself admire him. After all—*she smiled at the clinical flavor of her musings—*he is a fine specimen of a man, with a strong, manly face, bright gray-green eyes and shiny black hair. And he's saved from being too handsome by a barely-there scar on his chin.*

It's all right to think he's handsome, Casey reminded herself, *just remember he's not part of your plans.* She carefully began a catalog of his shortcomings, beginning with his lack of education and ending with his lack of interest in the more civilized things of life—culture, theater, good books, commitment, marriage.

Marriage? Casey bristled. Her thoughts really were going too far. Maybe it was the reduction of oxygen that occurred as the plane headed for higher and higher altitudes!

"I'll have us back at the cabin in about ten more minutes," Leon said, over the drone of the engine. "That's a lot better than the Land Rover, I bet."

She nodded and turned her attention back to the unbroken natural beauty below.

Just then, the engine coughed, abruptly portending disaster.

"What was that?" Casey asked, her eyes suddenly widening with fear.

Leon shook his head, a forced smile on his face. He checked the round, fluorescent gauges in front of him, and again, the engine protested, the wings diving and rolling like a carousel gone mad.

The plane jerked and sputtered in the air, and at last, the engine died, leaving them in an unnatural, eerie quiet, broken only by the whistling of wind as it wrapped around the plane.

"What's happening?" Casey demanded.

"It's a fuel-injector problem," Leon said, losing his nonchalant tone. He pumped the throttle several times, to no avail. "We'll have to land without the engine, if I can't keep her nose up long enough to find level ground. I've landed a plane without an engine before," he said, desperately trying to calm her fears even as he stared in disbelief at the gauges and switches that had, maddeningly, blinked off. "We're close enough to Skip's it shouldn't make a difference."

"We have no engine?"

Casey watched him in disbelief, her fingers icy cold from the shock, grasping the locket she wore every day, the locket with her picture of Joseph. Her throat tightened and she struggled for every breath. *Lord, don't take me away from my baby,* she prayed. *Don't let him grow up without parents, too.*

"Don't worry, I can bring her down. Look! There's the cabin," Leon said, pointing down to the familiar, pine-circled plain.

"What will you do?" she asked, reaching out to touch his sleeve.

"You have to trust that I know what I'm doing," he said. "My plane has always been in great condition—and I'm counting on that to pull us through."

But she saw the fear that etched his face. He wasn't very confident. How could he be? An engine dead. She sat back and grimly watched the ground rising to meet them. It felt strange, somehow beautiful if it wasn't so dangerous, to be gliding above the earth, accompanied only by the ghostly song of the wind.

Leon flipped on the radio. The silence was interrupted with electronic hissing. He was instantly grateful he had installed a battery that separately fed the radio. Most airplanes lose their radio contact as soon as the engine dies, but Leon was a careful pilot, constantly updating the condition of his plane, constantly watchful for yet another way to improve it.

Now he hoped that every margin of safety and care he had installed would work in his favor. Hoped that his luck—added to his careful planning and long record of working on his plane—would be good.

"Skip, can you read me? This is Leon, you remember—Casey's flyboy," Leon spoke into the receiver.

The hissing continued, for a second uninterrupted, and for an instant, Leon despaired, thinking that his radio wouldn't help them, that they would be on their own.

"Yeah, but I'm...not hearing...an engine," Skip said. He sounded so far away, so inaccessible, so fuzzy. But Leon's face brightened, and he knew that his irascible confidence was back. Some would call it arrogance, the same confidence that had carried him throughout his life.

"We've got a little fuel-injection problem," Leon said, his voice suddenly relaxed. "We'll try to land a little up-plain from you. We need you to come pick us up when we do."

"I read you," Skip responded.

Casey felt the hot terror rise in her throat, and it was accompanied by another, more consuming emotion—anger. She couldn't know of Leon's careful attention to his plane's condition; she only heard the cockiness in his voice as he continued to banter with Skip, little knowing that that chatter was important in locating his exact position with relationship to the cabin. Convinced that the plane's engine failure was Leon's fault, she was unable to believe that there were things in this world utterly out of the control of mere mortals. As the anger overwhelmed her, giving her an uncanny courage, she wanted to grab the radio's microphone and call to Skip. *Tell my boy I love him,* she thought.

She tried a trick that she had used when she had first lost her mother and she didn't want anyone to know that she was afraid or angry or confused at the lack of love she felt from others. She pretended she was someone else, someone braver, someone who could look death straight in the eye without flinching.

"We'll circle a few times, letting the plane naturally drop," Leon said to both Skip and Casey. "The snowfall yesterday will really help. The difference will be like falling on plush carpeting instead of a hardwood floor."

Skip signed off, and Leon switched off the radio, preparing himself with unshakable, grim concentration for the work ahead.

The plane whirled in long circles, drifting downward like a piece of paper. They glided closer and closer to the ground.

"We'll land on this turn," Leon said. "Brace yourself."

She put her arms around her head protectively and leaned forward. She felt the plane dipping, so slowly as to almost not be moving. Then she heard Leon shout, and the plane shattered to the ground, plowing through the snow, the cockpit convulsing with a scraping of metal and ice and immovable earth.

This is what it's like to die, she gasped, squeezing her eyes shut.

The plane shuddered forward, shaking Casey so hard she thought her body was ripping apart.

But it wasn't death.

It was too quiet.

At last, she realized the plane had stopped. They weren't moving. The air was silent. She wasn't dead. She lifted up her head.

"Hot dog!" Leon whooped. "I've never made such a great landing!"

She looked at him, assessing his apparent devil-may-care attitude, missing the shiver of relief that coursed through his muscles.

"I'm supposed to be *happy?*" she demanded bitterly, feeling the reflexive shaking of her shoulders as her body released its pent-up tension. "You take me out on a rattle-trap plane and when we don't get killed, you want congratulations!"

She kicked open her door and jumped from the plane into the ankle-high drift of snow. She shivered when the icy cold chill reached up under her jeans, soaking the bottom of her long underwear.

Leon's own pent-up tension erupted.

"Hey, lady, I didn't ask for a Nobel Prize. I'm just telling you it was a good landing," he said, leaning over the passenger seat. "It was just a damn good landing."

"Well, congratulations, and get off my property."

She slammed the door, nearly smashing his face. Luckily she could see the Land Rover speeding toward her. She couldn't wait to see her son again, to kiss his soft face, to know that she hadn't been taken from him, to know that he hadn't been consigned to the same life she had led.

"What do you mean get off your property?" Leon yelled after her, jumping down from his seat on the plane.

"I mean, don't come back, you're off the job, fired, terminated, whatever word it takes to get you to understand I don't want you around," she cried, turning.

The Land Rover had stopped alongside her. She yanked open the passenger door. Skip sat in the driver's seat, with Joseph, who had been hastily arranged in his car seat, beside him. She jumped in next to her son, smothered his face with a grateful kiss and fell back, relieved.

"Take me home," she said.

"But what about Leon?" Skip asked.

The flyboy rushed to the Land Rover and pounded on the passenger side.

"Let me in!" he demanded.

Skip leaned over Casey and flipped open the passenger seat.

"Get on in and scrunch yourself up in the back seat," he said wearily. "I guess I would be a pretty lowdown skunk to let you stew out here in your own juices."

They drove back to the cabin in silence. As soon as Skip stopped the Land Rover, Casey flung open her car door, grabbed her startled baby and ran into the cabin without a backward glance.

Damn him, she thought to herself, sinking into the porcelain tub and letting the steaming water rise to cover her breasts.

Endangering her life with his ramshackle plane. And that cocky manner of his! Uneducated, uncultured—couldn't hold a candle to Robert. Maybe the most infuriating thing was that she had found him so attractive, so handsome in an uncivilized sort of way. She smiled when she thought how uncomfortable he'd look in a tuxedo—or even an ordinary suit—but she had to admit he sure made a pair of jeans and a flannel shirt look unbelievably sexy.

But the smile disappeared when she remembered how she had talked so freely with him as they had flown out to the settlement, even more freely than she would have with Skip, and she thought of Skip as the next best thing to a grandfather. She searched for an explanation of why she had opened up to him, talking about the past. I was afraid, she remembered. I was so scared in that plane that I just lost my head and my defenses. And those thoughts brought her around in a perfect circle; she was back to railing against the flyboy for his plane, his arrogance, his handsomeness.

She stopped her brooding for a moment to listen for Joseph. He was happily playing in the playpen in his bedroom, just off the bathroom. Although he could not yet talk, he babbled loudly, mimicking the cadence of adult conversation. No doubt he was explaining some fine point of the baby world to one of his teddy bears.

Casey smiled again, remembering the sheer joy of having been granted a pardon by death and leaned back in the tub, luxuriating in the steaming water.

She heard the commotion at the bottom of the stairs— Skip and Leon were arguing. Casey couldn't hear precisely what they were saying and she strained her ears to listen. They were coming up the stairs!

She jumped up from the bathtub and jerked a towel around her body. She looked for her clothes and then remembered with a start that she had taken them downstairs to the washing machine. Before she could reach her bathrobe, which was lying in the bedroom, the bathroom door swung open and she was face-to-face with Leon Brodie.

He stood, hand still planted on the doorknob, as surprised as she. Like boxers in the ring, they stared at each other, each convinced the other was an aggressive and unyielding combatant.

"What are you doing in here?" Casey demanded, with a defensive tone that should have persuaded Leon to turn tail and run.

"I'm sorry," he said, shifting his gaze away from her as she struggled with her towel, but making no movement to leave. "I thought this door led to your bedroom. I didn't mean to walk in." His eyes remained resolutely fastened on a distant point somewhere beyond the medicine cabinet. "I just wanted to tell you that I've heard about your husband... I'm very sorry about what happened to him."

Through the open door, she could see Skip, sheepishly turning to walk down the stairs. His guilty eyes had refused to meet hers and she knew what that old man had done. He had told Leon about Robert's accident!

She wondered, with a touch of anger tempered only by her long affection for Skip, what else he had decided to tell Leon.

"I just wanted you to know that there's nothing I can do about your husband, there's nothing I can do about how scared you were," Leon continued softly, his eyes—liquid and wide open—taking in the full length of her body, from the damp curls on her head to the drops of water on her toes. "I'm sorry about how flip I acted about the landing."

He swallowed, hard and strenuously, as his eyes lingered on the curve of her shoulder, at the rapidly fluttering pulse point at the base of her throat, at the hint of a dark line of flesh that separated the breasts tightly bound with terry-cloth towel.

She stared at him, struggling to catch her breath. She could smell him, that musky odor of masculinity. She opened her mouth to gulp in air and felt her lips become dry and parched.

He stepped toward her; now he was only inches away from her, his large, callused hands held awkwardly at his sides. As if not holding her was the most unnatural thing in the world.

"Don't you feel it?" he asked, his face demanding and sensual, yet somehow devoid of the boyish cockiness she had found so annoying.

"Feel what?" Casey's voice cracked.

She looked at him warily. She sensed the difficulty he had in restraining himself, in holding back the fire storm.

"You know what I'm talking about," he answered, his voice rough with emotion.

But, suddenly, her surrender to him was cut short by a tightening panic—a remembrance of her past with Robert, of the tender lies she had told in order to prop up his masculine ego. She didn't have, had never had, the capacity to give in to passion, to give in to love and the senses.

"We've only known each other for a day, not even quite twenty-four hours," she said, startled by the primness that had entered her voice, trying to forget their first meeting.

"Casey, does it matter if it's twenty-four hours or twenty-four days, twenty-four months or twenty-four years? What matters is what we feel."

"And just what is that?" she challenged, squaring her arms in front of her chest.

He started to speak, his mouth struggling to say the words. At last he gave up, and dragging her into his arms, kissed her, pulling her mouth to his. She gave a tremor of resistance, but she had been hungry too long. She parted her lips, tentatively letting the swelling emotion take her away.

As she lost her breath, as she lost her balance, as she lost her resolve—and just as her body prepared to surrender— she jerked away. Leon, baffled, by her sudden dismissal, stared at her questioningly.

"Stop...I don't know what Joseph's doing," she whispered, desperately floundering for an excuse to run, to escape from the threat posed by his kisses. "I have to check on him."

Leon released her and she looked into the playpen to see that Joseph had fallen asleep, arms enveloping his teddy. Casey felt Leon standing behind her. He caressed her back and reached his arms around her waist.

"I can't do this," she whispered. "I can't get involved with you."

"Why?" he asked, nudging her breasts with his strong, capable hands.

"You're not part of my future," she answered. "You're just someone I have nothing in common with, someone I don't even like." She whirled around and stared at him. "I'd be happy if you walked right out of here right now and I never saw you again."

"Because I'm an uneducated, unwashed, uncultured flyboy?" he asked. "Because I don't measure up to your expectations about a real man with a fancy degree and a membership in the Great Books series?"

She started to protest as his rancorous words seemed to expose her for being some sort of a snob. Wasn't it more complicated than that? Wasn't it that Robert was everything she thought a man should be: educated, cultured, accomplished? As if being the smartest and most capable scholar gave a man the power to make sense of a sometimes cruel and irrationally lonely world?

Besides, would she have to enter into a whole new deception, or worse, would she be able to give herself to this virtual stranger in a way that she hadn't been able to give herself to her own husband?

"Yes," she admitted, lifting her chin with resolve. "You're not the kind of man I could ever get involved with."

He entwined his fingers with hers, with a damnable look of amusement on his face.

"Are you telling me it's just business between you and me?" His tone was light and teasing, but Casey could feel the dangerous undercurrents.

She nodded grimly, desperately hoping he wouldn't challenge her with another of his kisses—and desperately hoping he would. For a moment, he towered over her, seeming to weigh his alternatives. Then a mask of coldness came over him.

"If that's what you want," he said curtly, and let himself out the bathroom door without a backward glance.

When Casey woke, she checked the clock—6:00 a.m. She felt the emptiness of the bed as a coldness that was worse than usual. The bedside lamp was on, the discarded textbook lay on her lap. It had been a hard night. And though she could have gladly gone back to sleep now, Joseph was crying.

She went to get him, thankful for the simplicity of the love she felt for her baby, and that he gave to her.

She tried not to think of the complications that Leon posed for her, from the transportation of the exhibit pieces to the personal complications that meant so much more to her.

A single kiss had changed things for her. She may have said it was business, but in her gut she knew she was wrong. And maybe she needed to talk about it with him.

Leon's kiss had done something to her, something that had made it nearly impossible to sleep. She had studied a complex text on anthropological statistical analysis, hoping the erudite work would engage her so that she could forget him. She shivered when she thought of the feelings he had evoked. And she felt guilty.

It had never been like that with Robert.

Casey had known she was something of a cold fish even before she married. There were two men, boys really, she had "seen." One in high school, the last few months of her senior year. Another at the University of Chicago. Both had kissed her—she had never let them do more—and she had never felt . . . well, anything.

With Robert, she had assumed that the fact that his kisses didn't make her swoon with delight was surely her fault. And when they made love, she didn't respond the way either of them would have liked. Surely if she loved him, it would get better, she had thought.

But after a few months, she had resigned herself to the fact that she was a cold, unreachable woman. She deceived Robert, letting him think that she had changed, had developed a passion to match his own.

She knew she would never be a professional actress, but she had thought that her performances had been enough to fool Robert.

But the way Skip talked, it sounded as if her acting may not have been too convincing. And now this flyboy's kiss threatened to make her see her frigidity as having more to do with Robert than with herself.

It had taken her breath away, leaving her baffled and bewitched, hungry for more. Maybe if she made love to him and experienced the frustrations she had felt with Robert, or knew him long enough to know in her heart that he was just an ordinary man, her reactions would cool.

But for now, she replayed that kiss over and over, until she thought she might burst with anticipation of another.

She'd have to be on her guard with him, starting now, Casey thought, as she slipped on her jeans.

Picking up Joseph, she ran downstairs to the kitchen. Skip was seated at the table, reading glasses perched on his nose, working on the crossword puzzle that he had started a month before.

"Where's Leon?" she asked, hoping there was some casualness in her voice.

"Gone," Skip said. "He's gone."

"Where?" Casey asked, feeling her mouth go dry.

"He's gone, he left, he took his plane, you've lost your flyboy. He's not coming back," Skip said. "You don't happen to know a fourteen-letter word for 'let down,' do you?"

Casey turned away, holding Joseph just a little more tightly. She hoped Skip couldn't see the very real disappointment on her face.

Chapter Six

With concentration honed by years of flying, Leon checked his instrument panel, reading each gauge once, and then a second time. Satisfied, he gave a quick wave to the kid standing at the nose of the plane.

"Give her a spin!" Leon shouted.

The youth, a sullen, stuffy-nosed boy wearing a sealskin parka, gave a shove to Leon's plane's nose propeller. The propeller twirled and then its blades disappeared in the blur of high-speed motion, the whine momentarily reminding Leon of cicada summers in Alabama. The engine's force rattled the insides of the plane, rippling the coffee that Leon had precariously balanced on the second seat. Leon waved again at the boy, who had trotted out onto a muddy bank of muskegon. Leon maneuvered the plane toward the open strip of land that served as a primitive runway.

"Thanks," he mouthed to the boy with a thumbs-up signal that the boy, an Alaskan native who had seen too many planes, merely nodded at.

With his free hand, Leon adjusted the plastic lid on the cup of coffee he had bought at the makeshift fill-up station. It was amazing what a good meal and a cup of coffee could do for a man, Leon thought, feeling refreshed.

He was four hours away from Casey, nearly five hundred miles through central Alaska, nearly at the Anchorage airport Calvin Dodge used as headquarters for the transport business. Though closer geographically to his buddy, it was Casey he was mesmerized by.

And that kiss—a kiss that had settled on his memory in a way that made the countless women he'd encountered in his life disappear into a murky fog.

She couldn't tell him she wasn't feeling anything.

The shoe that he had comfortably worn with every other woman he had ever met was now on another foot. Casey felt attracted to him, she couldn't hide that. He knew there were undercurrents of passion that she was only dimly aware of. But she didn't want a relationship with him, taking the role of reluctant involvement that had formerly been his domain.

Damn—he could see why women sometimes became so infuriated with him.

There was an important difference between Casey and how Leon had acted in the arena of romantic conquest: for a woman like Casey, he knew she wouldn't act on passion without there being a valid foundation of love and commitment.

He had to get out, before he did something foolish— something insane. Next thing you knew, he was going to be like Calvin, infuriatingly married!

He had never had any trouble leaving women. He had known a lot of women who had wanted him to stick around, thinking they could "tame" him. He had perfected the skill of walking out each woman's door without a moment of regret.

But this woman was different. Maybe it was because she didn't seem to want anything from him. She hadn't developed a game plan for snaring him, she hadn't tried to twist him around her little finger. She had come to him gently, honestly, as if she had been stripped of any feminine armor.

He had decided long ago that he wasn't the type for settling down. He loved the sky too much—and how could you ask a woman to share that? Especially a woman like Casey. Especially with that little baby. Especially when she probably wanted evenings at home reading books and discussing opera.

That was part of the problem, really.

There had never been a woman who had stripped him down to his most basic insecurities. And Casey could do it with the most offhand phrases.

She had made him feel so damn small, with the simple tilt of her chin as she had pointed out to him that he didn't have half of what her big-shot professor husband had had. She had brought him face-to-face with his most basic insecurity—that he was a failure. He had always told himself that he was superior to the average man who tied himself down with a wife and child and job and such. And he had always told himself that he could succeed at those things—marriage, family, career—if he had wanted them. But the doubts had become more profound with each passing year, and Casey, with infuriating ease, had exploded his most private delusions and had brought him to the brink of viewing his life as a string of failures.

And now, up in the air, a new tank of gas in the plane and a good breakfast in himself, Leon grimly sipped his coffee. He set his eyes on the mountainous horizon and tried to remember how much he truly loved the sky. Suddenly the choices he had made about his life, the very ones that had seemed so noble and manly, seemed silly, hollow, even cowardly. But he didn't want to think like this. He touched the throttle, easing the plane higher into the quiet sky.

She hated him. There was no doubt about it—she hated him. He had taken advantage of her—played with her emotions—and left her in a lurch.

She'd give anything to have him back—not so she could put her arms around him or kiss him once again, she just wanted to wring his neck.

"What are you so steamed about?" Skip asked, coming into the kitchen. "You've been slamming the cabinet doors like you're using Morse code to talk to someone a mile away."

She stood in the middle of the kitchen, holding a can of soup in one hand and a can opener in the other.

"I'm just making a bowl of soup," she said. "Do you mind?"

He shook his head and started to leave.

"Skip!"

He turned around. "What's the problem?"

"Skip, I kissed him last night," she admitted, putting her soup can and opener on the counter and slumping into one of the chairs. A simple sentence hadn't communicated the range of contradictory emotions she felt, and Skip's good-natured yet derisive look convinced her that he didn't understand.

"Shh, Joseph may be taking his nap, but he's a little young for this racy stuff," Skip said, and held a finger to his lips. "You sure come up with interesting secrets."

"And now he's gone."

"I'm not surprised by that. He strikes me as the kind of guy who would want to move on," Skip said, and with a sly shift of his eyes, he continued. "Especially if you weren't all that friendly."

"I feel terrible," she said, trying desperately to make sense of the situation. Was she hurt because Leon didn't share the unexpected feelings she did, or was she angry because she wasn't sure she could make it to Chicago now?

Skip turned a chair around and sat down, his legs flanking either side of the chair back.

"What did you expect? That he'd suddenly put on a three-piece suit, get an academic job and go buy tickets to a Vivaldi concert?"

"I wanted him to stick around," she cried, feeling the tears fall down her cheeks.

Skip pulled his chair close to hers and put his hand on her shoulder.

"You wanted someone to stick around," he said quietly. "It's tough to be left behind, whether it's by a husband, a lover, or even parents."

She nodded, not daring to look at him because of the tears gathering at the rim of her eyes.

"Stop your blubbering," Skip said, pulling a handkerchief from a back pocket. "You have a museum to get to— aren't you supposed to give your little talk on Friday?"

Friday? Suddenly Casey felt herself dropped down to earth. There were matters that were a lot more important than whether her feelings had been hurt by a rude flyboy. She had four hundred pounds of exhibit material to transport to Chicago, a museum exhibition to set up, a lecture to prepare, countless interviews to give and all the responsibilities of a real professional. She wiped her tears and tried to focus on the present, straightening in her seat.

"I think I have only one choice, if you can live with it," she said. "I've got to take the Land Rover. If I push off today, I've got a shot at making Anchorage by Tuesday."

"You'll never make it," Skip said, shaking his head. "We've been over this so many times. Maybe you can get everything in the Land Rover, but the problem is the driving. There's nearly a thousand miles of twisted road between here and Anchorage. If it was easy driving, I'd think you'd have a shot. But it's all gravel. That's tough driving."

It was true. Even the major Alaskan highways were gravel. Any other surface would be destroyed by the icy winter cold.

"Besides—" he paused "—what will you do about Joseph? I don't mind caring for him, but I think the little guy will miss you."

"But I'd take him with me," Casey said, surprised at his question.

"A six-month-old on a two- or three-day road trip? You're crazy."

Casey's shoulders slumped. Skip was right, of course. The idea of taking her baby and keeping him in the car seat for a cross-country trip was cruel and thoughtless. Little Joseph couldn't spend hour after hour strapped into a vinyl prison.

"Skip, what am I going to do? I can't leave my baby for a week, and I can't get another pilot on such short notice. Calvin had to work so hard to track down this one."

Skip shrugged.

"I don't know," he said finally. "I just don't know. I wish I was more help. If I were a younger man, I would take the load myself."

"Maybe I should call Harry," Casey said. "Ask him to loan me money to use one of the more expensive courier services—and put off the opening for a few days." She didn't look forward to the conversation. She knew Harry had had to pull some strings in order to get her the sizable honorarium in the first place, and the date of the opening had been set up months ago. Dear Harry had arranged everything—interviews, publicity, museum space—so that she could just breeze in at the last minute.

Harry had worked to create a fiction between them—that the university, the anthropology department, Harry himself, were so grateful and honored to have Casey's lecture and the Athabascan artifacts that what Harry had done to put this together was a treat for him. But Casey knew better. It couldn't be as simple as that. Instead, she believed Harry was working hard to honor his friend Robert, and to help his friend's widow put the memory of her husband behind her.

Casey couldn't, in her wildest imagination, suppose that Harry was doing this because her work was in any way exceptional, because her work in any way matched the work that Robert would have done, because she was not anywhere as good an anthropologist as her dead husband had been.

It was a favor—a huge favor—that Harry was granting by letting her have an exhibit, a lecture hall, a forum for presenting her work. If she was lucky, and the lectures went well, the university might make her an offer to become a guest lecturer for the semester. And then, an offer to become an assistant professor!

To encroach on Harry any further, to ask such a personal thing as a loan to hire one of the more expensive couriers—even assuming one could be had at this late date—was hard for her to contemplate.

"I don't really think you have a choice," Skip interrupted her thoughts. "You know, this might not be the time to bring this up but well, there's no secret—I've loved you like I would a daughter, and this boy, Joseph, he's like a grandson I'm never going to have. Maybe you should give up on this exhibit, and on this idea of moving away. Maybe you should think about making your life right here—even marrying again."

Casey started to protest, but he cut her off.

"You think that going to Chicago will solve all your problems. You think it's really your home. But you can't persuade me that Chicago is 'home' just because for four years you had a dorm room there."

"But it's where I lived the longest," Casey said, her lips tightened with anger. "And that's where I met Robert."

"Yeah, but you're not going to be comfortable in the city. There's hustle and bustle, there are crowds, it's never quiet and the traffic is terrible. Don't you remember any of that?"

"Yeah," Casey said warily, although in truth, she couldn't remember much about Chicago, least of all the bad parts. "But how do you know what Chicago's like?"

Skip burst into laughter. "Because you complained about it so much when you first moved here."

Casey smiled and the tension between them dissipated.

"Don't you remember the first time you and Robert swam in the lake out back, by yourselves with no one else around? Or the first time you saw the caribou over the fields? Or how happy you were when you knew you didn't have to worry about locking your door at night? And I think you've forgotten the real pleasure you get from cataloging those old Indian stories,'' Skip said, giving her an unexpected, gruff compliment about the commitment she had to her work. "Do you think there's any Indian settlements in the middle of Chicago where you can crank up your tape recorder and immerse yourself in a primitive culture?''

They both smiled wryly at his last question.

"But if Chicago isn't my home, where is?'' Casey asked softly.

"I swear, Casey, if you can't figure that one out, I'm not going to tell you." And he turned without another word to go into the living room and play Joplin on the piano.

"You're retiring your plane?'' Calvin Dodge exclaimed, slamming the smoky-glassed office door behind him. "That plane is the finest twin-seater in the country.''

"It has the worst fuel-injection in the country, too,'' Leon said, putting his boots squarely on Calvin's desk and leaning back in his chair, and thinking, with brief bitterness, of how the fuel-injection system had been the cause of some, but by no means all, of his problems with Casey. "The plane's a collector's item, that's for sure, but I think her flying days are over.''

Calvin dropped his soft, plump body onto his desk chair and pulled on his glasses. His rabbitlike eyes seemed, as always, unnaturally small behind the lenses.

"Leon Brodie retiring his plane,'' Calvin said, letting out a low whistle. "I almost think I should call one of the news-wire services. I thought you'd never let that baby stay down on the ground for more than a day or two. When we were riding the circuit...''

"When we were riding the circuit, that plane was fifteen years younger, with a little more spunk than now," Leon reminded him.

"Well, she's still a beauty," Calvin said, by way of consolation. He squinted at Leon. "Now why don't you tell me what she's like."

"Come again?"

"Casey Stevens."

"Casey Stevens?" Leon felt his face flush with embarrassment. He had never been all that good at hiding things—one of the reasons why Calvin had never lost a game of poker to him. And, apparently, one of the reasons Calvin now had a conspiratorial look on his face.

Calvin opened the bottom left drawer of his desk and produced a bottle of liquor and two paper cups.

"Want some?"

Leon nodded and Calvin poured.

"Look, this kind of thing has to involve a woman," Calvin said, reaching across the desk to hand Leon a full glass. "When we were young, I never expected I'd have any success with women. I'm fat, I can't see worth a damn and I certainly don't look like anything from *Gentlemen's Quarterly*." He waved away Leon's token protest. "It's true, you know it." He took a swig from his glass. "I never thought I'd end up with Belinda. I'll tell you a secret," he said, lowering his voice conspiratorially. He could scarcely be heard above the roar of an incoming plane. "I got into this business for her. She doesn't know it, but I would have ended up staying a flyboy just like you. But I took one look at her, and I changed my ways. I lost fifteen pounds—I don't eat chocolate bars for breakfast anymore, and I stopped drinking milk directly out of the carton."

Leon nodded, remembering the changes that had come over his friend nearly five years before.

But Calvin wasn't finished praising his wife and unwittingly added the one sentence sure to raise Leon's ire. "She's my best pilot, you know."

Leon sipped from his cup, resisting the urge to challenge the statement, and waited for the bellow of an incoming airplane to die down. Calvin's office was just off the runway, and sometimes it felt as though the planes were landing right on top of him.

"She's going to be your second best from now on," he said quietly, so that it wasn't until Calvin's smile broadened that Leon was sure that his own voice had carried over the roar of the planes.

Calvin burst into hearty laughter. He poured a second glass for himself and for Leon.

"That's great, I'm looking forward to it," he said. "If you weren't drinking, I'd send you up tonight."

Leon held his paper cup high in a token salute and drank from the burning liquid. He stood up and went to the window that overlooked the blinking lights of the airport.

"So what's Casey like? Like I said, there's always a woman involved. And when I asked you if you wouldn't mind flying her down to Chicago, I didn't have any idea of...well, you tell me what happened," Calvin persisted. "A man like you, and me, if you don't mind being put in the same category, only change for a reason. And that reason is always a woman."

Leon started to protest, but decided better of it. Instead he drained his whiskey.

"She's pretty," he said at last.

"I thought that might be the case—although the only time I've ever seen her she was nine months pregnant and not in a particularly pleasant mood."

"No, she's really pretty. She's very small, delicate, like some kind of doll...and she's got beautiful blue eyes. And she has reddish-brown hair, cut like one of those flappers from the twenties," said Leon with a shrug. "I don't know how to explain her."

"You're doing pretty good so far."

"Well, she's honest. In a way that makes you want to be honest with her. And she's soft in a way that makes you want to soften up. And she's passionate, although I have a hunch that passion is something that scares her."

"Does she love you?" Calvin asked.

Leon looked into the darkness, watching the blue, red and white blinking lights of the runway. A plane zoomed in overhead and the noise momentarily stopped his thoughts of Casey.

"How do you tell?" he asked, after the noise died down. He could hardly believe himself. Leon Brodie, asking advice about women from Calvin Dodge?

"I didn't know, and so I asked Belinda to marry me," Calvin admitted. "After I asked her at least six or seven times, she said yes. I guess that meant she loved me. Until then I didn't have a clue."

"I don't think I'm quite ready for that," Leon said.

Calvin sensed the resoluteness that had entered Leon's voice.

"Want to see her, by the way?" Calvin asked, pulling a wallet from his back pocket. "You could come home with me for dinner. Besides, you haven't seen David in a while—here, let me show you his latest picture."

Leon walked over and took the wallet photograph from Calvin. As he stared at the carbon copy of Calvin, right down to the black plastic frame glasses, he wondered about himself. Would there be a Leon a year from now who would pull a picture of Casey and Joseph from his pocket? He rejected the thought and pushed the photograph back to Calvin.

"I don't want to just be a pilot," he said. "I want part of the business. And I've got the money for it. My father left me some and I've been waiting for the right moment to invest."

"You really are serious about her."

"Look, Calvin, if I never saw her again, it would probably be for the best. She's the kind of woman who drowns a man," he said, feeling an irrational anger about the last vestiges of freedom slipping away from him. "But I'm getting old. You can't fly every day not knowing where you're going to sleep that night. Wears you out. When I left her this morning, I told myself I was never going back. By the time I got here, I couldn't wait to see her again. I've never needed anyone. And now..."

"I understand," Calvin murmured. "I'd be dropping off Belinda at the end of a date, and I'd miss her already."

"So I want in on the business," Leon continued, sitting down again. "And I want one favor, but no questions asked."

"Sure, you know whatever it is..."

"I want a plane, a six-seater, for a week."

"She's that important?"

"Yeah," Leon said, his feelings confused. He felt embarrassed that a woman could mean so much to him. On the other hand he felt pride—he was going to come through for someone...someone special. "Sometimes I feel like I'm flying blind," he started, trying to articulate to his friend the enormous conflicts within him. "I'm flying blind in a foggy night with my instrument panel out and not a lot of ideas as to where I'm going."

"That's the way it always is," Calvin said.

The two men stared silently out at the late-afternoon sky.

"Can I tell Belinda to set another place for dinner?" Calvin asked, brightly returning their thoughts to the comradely relationship they had always enjoyed. "She's going to be happy you're joining the business, but I think she might fight you on who's the better pilot."

"I promise not to tell her she's second best until after she feeds us."

Calvin stood up and held out his right hand.

"I want to meet her again someday, Leon."

Leon smiled and took Calvin's hand in a vigorous handshake.

"I'd like that," he said. "That is, if she's not so mad at me that I'm never going to have a chance to talk to her again. She probably wants to wring my neck."

Chapter Seven

"Casey, Casey, wake up!"

Casey reluctantly opened her eyes, and her fingers involuntarily released a sheaf of ponderous research papers she had been reading. They fluttered like snowflakes to the woven rag rug. The late-afternoon fire had gone cold and dark, so that for a moment she thought it was already night. Skip stood in front of her, impatiently waving his hands.

What was that buzzing noise? She shook her head and yawned.

"It's not Joseph, is it?" she asked, groggily trying to push the buzzing from her head.

"No, he's fine. He's upstairs napping in his playpen," Skip said. "Can't you hear it?"

"The buzzing? That's not just me?"

"No, he's come back," Skip exclaimed. "It's him and he's got your plane—a real six-seater, twin-engine turbo. He's come back."

NO COST! NO OBLIGATION TO BUY!
NO PURCHASE NECESSARY!

PLAY "LUCKY 7"
AND GET AS MANY AS SIX FREE GIFTS...

HOW TO PLAY:

1. With a coin, carefully scratch off the silver box at the right. This makes you eligible to receive one or more free books, and possibly other gifts, depending on what is revealed beneath the scratch-off area.

2. You'll receive brand-new Silhouette Romance™ novels. When you return this card, we'll send you the books and gifts you qualify for *absolutely free!*

3. If we don't hear from you, every month we'll send you 6 additional novels to read and enjoy. You can return them and owe nothing but if you decide to keep them, you'll pay only $2.25* per book, a saving of 25¢ each off the cover price. There is **no** extra charge for postage and handling. There are **no** hidden extras.

4. When you join the Silhouette Reader Service™, you'll get our subscribers'-only newsletter, as well as additional free gifts from time to time, just for being a subscriber.

5. You must be completely satisfied. You may cancel at any time simply by sending us a note or a shipping statement marked ''cancel'' or by returning any shipment to us at our cost.

*Terms and prices subject to change without notice.
Sales tax applicable in N.Y.
© 1990 HARLEQUIN ENTERPRISES LIMITED

This lovely Victorian pewter-finish miniature is perfect for displaying a treasured photograph—and it's yours absolutely free—when you accept our no-risk offer.

Skip didn't need to say who. Casey bolted upright. He's back? She had spent the past day paralyzed with terror, hesitating every time she tried to get up her nerve to call Harry, to tell him that she couldn't come through, to tell him that Robert's museum exhibit would never be a reality. Obsessively she questioned her future—how would she ever get an academic job Outside if she couldn't finish the work on the exhibit? What if she was consigned, a failure, to Alaska forever?

And now he was back?

"Let's go!" Skip threw her parka at her. He yanked on his own jacket and opened the front door. The *whoosh!* of cold air brought Casey to life. She hastily drew the parka around her shoulders and followed Skip out into the frozen, snowy plain. The buzzing had become a roar, and she looked up to the skies and saw the hawklike body of a King-Aire six-seater plane. It shot across the sky and pulled a clean, sharp arc.

"He's in for a landing!" Skip shouted, his voice barely rising above the din.

The charcoal-colored plane circled back to the plain, slowing to a glide. It dropped its wheels and the flaps pulled up. The roar deepened and became high-pitched. The snow swirled around Casey's feet, sucked by the force of the plane. The plane's wheels touched the ground, the body bumped and, for a moment as it bolted across the plain, the plane appeared to gain speed. At last the brakes won out and the plane stopped, not a hundred feet from the cabin.

Casey shook her hair free of wind-scattered snowflakes and stared, half disbelieving, at the plane now parked at her doorstep.

"Come on, slowpoke," Skip demanded, dragging her after him.

In the excitement of the plane's appearance, she hadn't thought how she felt about seeing Leon again. Her feelings of anger about his desertion had solidified in the past day. He had left her in the lurch, scared her into believing that her dreams—every moment of a future she had wanted so desperately—were forever to be out of reach. All because of his abandonment—although in her most depressed moments, she remembered that it had been she who had told him he was fired.

She hung back from Skip's excited gait.

"Skip, I think I should go back and check on Joseph," she said simply. "He could be getting into all kinds of trouble."

"He's in his playpen, he'll be fine for a minute."

Skip firmly gripped her arm, pulling her along with him as if he were dragging an oversize piece of luggage toward the gray cruiser.

Up ahead, the plane's cabin door swung open and a face—familiar even with dark aviator glasses and baseball cap—peered out. Even at a distance of fifty feet, Casey could see that Leon still had the cockiness and boyish arrogance that had unnerved her so.

But worse, he had the same sizzling masculinity that had made him such a threat to her.

Casey's heartbeat quickened. Damn him! It wasn't fair that he could still look so good, so sexy, so exciting to her! She had wanted to forget that moment in the bedroom. That kiss; she bristled at the memory of unfamiliar sensations, a memory that was not tainted with her confused, ambivalent anger.

"Leon!" Skip exclaimed. "Great to see you. How'd you end up with this rig?"

Leon stretched his hand out to Skip. Casey hung back, hoping to melt into the afternoon shadows behind Skip.

How could she face him when it seemed as if he held the key to her inner core?

After exchanging a greeting with Skip, he casually handed his flight bag to the older man and jumped to the ground.

"Hello, boss lady, ready to fly?" he asked, letting his eyes lazily move over her. Casey scrambled for her breath and looked away.

"Your coming here is a little..." Without meaning to, she sounded brisk and irritable, as if she were a schoolteacher scolding an errant pupil.

"Maybe it's a little unexpected?" Leon supplied, with a quick, damning wink in Skip's direction.

He retrieved his bag from Skip and took her arm. Casey felt herself being transported against her will, as if by an avalanche, as the three of them headed for the cabin.

"You've got to be in Chicago by Friday," Leon continued, his Alabama accent all the more noticeable. "How about loading up tonight, after y'all feed me some dinner? We could make a lot of headway if we got started early."

"I'll put some salmon steaks out for you," Skip said, ignoring the look Casey gave him. "And Casey here can help you load."

Casey yanked her arm out from Leon's grip. She started to speak, to protest, to disapprove, but Skip quickly opened the door and ushered the two of them into the warm, woody-smelling cabin.

"This calls for another celebration," Skip said. "It's great to have you back, Leon."

"It's hard to pass up the money," Leon said, an inscrutable smile passing over his face.

He didn't try to kiss me again, Casey thought to herself as she dragged the wooden crate out of the Land Rover trunk and pulled it onto her shoulders. He didn't say anything about that first kiss, and as a matter of fact, he didn't say much of anything else. That crack about the money! She could just kill him. Casey kicked the trunk of the Land Rover closed and shoved a full wooden crate through the plane's main cabin door.

"This is the last one," she said to Leon, who effortlessly picked it up and disappeared into the back of the plane's cabin. She had hoped that her purposely bland, expressionless tone would make him at least ask her what was wrong.

But, nothing. He acted as if walking out on her and appearing a few hours later as if nothing had happened was the most normal thing in the world.

But you fired him, a niggling voice in the back of her mind said.

"Yeah, and I kissed him, too," she said out loud.

"Huh?" Leon asked, raising a sweat-soaked face from his backbreaking job of loading the boxes and strapping each one down. "Did you say something?"

"No," Casey answered, shaking her head.

She spun and headed back toward the Land Rover.

"You bringing the crib next?" Leon shouted after her. She stopped and turned around. "I made room for you and Joseph at the front of the cabin. You'll want supplies, all that diaper stuff," he finished lamely, leaning his head out the doorway. She could see the twinkle of his eyes even in the dark.

"I've got all my personal belongings ready to load." Casey slid into her seat in the Land Rover. Was that all he had to say to her? Talking about diapers when he should be talking about love and relationships and...

As if nothing had happened.

Casey switched on the ignition and felt the rumbling power of the Land Rover's engine vibrate against her body. What had actually happened? she asked herself, trying her trick of thinking of herself as someone else, someone more sophisticated, someone braver in the face of passion. What was the big deal about a simple kiss?

She squared her shoulders, puckered her lips and kissed the air a few times.

"Now, what's so special about that?" she muttered. "Just two sets of lips pressed together—in some cultures such behavior wouldn't mean anything at all."

She tried to think of any cultures where kissing wasn't a part of the language of love and then decided that the real issue wasn't whether they had kissed, but whether she wanted it to be the start of something.

She turned on the headlights and started the short drive to the cabin. It wasn't as if she would want a relationship with someone like Leon. He wasn't what she had in mind. He wasn't well educated, they didn't share many interests, he wouldn't be a good father to Joseph—at least he said he wouldn't—and he certainly wouldn't be interested in moving to Chicago. She concentrated on creating a definitive list of the conflicts their relationship would entail—well, actually, she compiled a list of his faults.

So maybe it was all for the best, his silence, his lack of emotion.

Casey pulled the Land Rover to a stop and jumped from her seat onto the dirt path to the cabin. She opened the hotel door and breathed in the warm air.

Why would one kiss affect her so deeply, be so unexpected in its explosiveness? She shook her head, willing herself to forget it, just forget it. Just forget a simple touch on her own lips by the lips of another.

"Skip?" she called, dropping her parka by the roaring fireplace and bounding up the stairs. "Have you got Joseph ready to go?"

Somehow the sound of her own cheerful voice reminded her of the adventure she was about to begin. The university, the city, a new home, a place for Joseph to grow up, a future. The rest of her life opened up like a drama. She reached the top of the stairs, and stopped to catch her breath.

Skip stood in the hallway with Joseph in his arms, the little baby clinging to his beard. Joseph's eyes were droopy; he was nearing his bedtime. Casey felt a pang of guilt for taking him away from this place, because this really was his home. Joseph had never even spent a night away from the cabin.

But how could she raise a baby alone out here?

She took her baby from Skip's arms, slipping the coarse white beard out from between Joseph's pudgy fingers.

"Jeez, he's got a grip," Skip said, rubbing his face. "Kid's going to be a wrestler."

"First professor at the University of Chicago to be quarterback for the Bears," Casey replied, using the common joke they shared. Skip always thought Joseph was going to be a bruiser; Casey always hoped he'd be a thinker.

She shifted Joseph from one hip to the other, uncertain of what to say, grateful for the tender grip of her son's hand on her shoulder.

"Have a good trip, pardner," Skip said, rubbing Joseph's head. "Take care of your mom, and I'll see you sometime."

"Skip, you've been so . . ." Casey began.

He put his hand to her lips. "Don't get soft on me."

Casey looked away, biting her lip to focus her thoughts, to stop a maudlin show of emotion, to stop the tears.

"We'll come back—" she hesitated at what they both knew was a lie "—sometime real soon. In the meantime, is there anything I can mail back for you?"

"How about a pound of frango mints from Marshall Field's?" he asked, naming his favorite candy—a treat that they mailed away for each Christmas.

"You got it," she promised.

She followed him down to the living room. He put on Joseph's snowsuit, while she shrugged on her parka and looked around for any last papers she might have forgotten.

It was amazing to her that she had been able to pack all her belongings into a single suitcase, just as she had when she had left for college. Someday it would be nice to move and have to use a moving van, she thought.

Come to think of it, someday it would be nice to never have to move.

Satisfied that she had packed everything, she put Joseph into his car seat and got into the passenger seat next to Skip. He started the engine.

Her future, a future that she had planned since Robert's death, had finally begun.

Casey felt tired, a bone-tired that made her legs cramp, her head ache and her eyes itch. Her ears rang with the sound of the engine even after nearly hour-long breaks on the ground at small, private airports that Leon insisted upon every time he needed to refuel. Casey couldn't understand how he could manage, how he could keep the plane in the air long after she would have called it quits.

But she didn't really have a chance to ask him. When they were on the ground, she walked around with Joseph, or bought a snack at the airport diner. At the smaller airports, she would ask someone to drive her to the nearest convenience store, where she'd buy a soft drink and something for Leon.

And after hurried thanks, he would disappear.

Leon himself always was busy, directing the filling of the plane's fuel tanks, checking on the engine, the oil, the maps. And always there was an old friend at the airport, someone who hadn't seen Leon since whenever he had last passed through.

Casey was amazed at the men and women who knew this flyboy. And Leon remembered everyone who knew him. She was impressed and somehow moved when he asked after the children of men he hadn't seen in years, remembering their names and their ages, and even the problems, as well as the triumphs, they had been having at school. He cooed and exclaimed over every picture brought out of a man's wallet, convincingly assuring the proud owner that the child, wife, or dog was the most attractive Leon had seen in years. And before Casey had a chance to say anything, Leon would usher her back into the plane for another few hours of flight.

And the women! Casey knew it was irrational to be bothered by this, but the women at the airports, the counter personnel or the controllers, always flirted with Leon, twisting their hair or tilting their chins in beguiling ways while asking Leon when, oh when, he would be returning.

With significant, almost challenging, looks in Casey's direction.

The most charitable explanation of Leon's popularity with women was that he was simply an attentive, charming man. But Casey preferred another, more malevolent possibility—Leon had been true to his word, incapable of loyalty to any woman, determined to hang on to his "masculine freedom."

Add that to his list of faults, Casey thought on more than one occasion as she reminded herself that a relationship was out of the question, as she eased her hurt over his seeming lack of interest in her.

She stayed in the passenger cabin while they were flying. Joseph lay in his crib, which had been wedged behind the curtain that separated the main cabin from the pilot's seat. Casey sat over him, played with him when he was awake, frankly glad when he was asleep. In back of her, tied down with ropes and seat belts and anything else Skip had had available, were the artifacts Casey had so carefully gathered during the past year.

And in a few hours, she would be home—home in Chicago, where she had met Robert.

At the last airport, in Nebraska, she had called Harry to tell him that she would be arriving at Meig's Field, the small airport right on Lake Michigan.

She had always appreciated that Harry, alone among Robert's colleagues, had tried to make her feel welcome after their wedding. He had taken them to dinner, with a blond actress who boasted of several commercials and a walk-on in an afternoon soap.

At some point during the evening, Robert had excused himself for a moment and the blonde was concentrating on the menu. Harry chose that moment to reassure Casey that the university-wide snub she had experienced after marrying Robert would soon pass.

"It's just faculty wives being a little defensive or maybe just a little jealous," Harry had said. "The women are worried their own husbands will leave them for a cute co-ed."

"But I'm not cute, and Robert wasn't married," Casey had protested.

"Your first point is untrue and the second irrelevant," Harry said, winking at her, and instantly, she was filled with self-confidence.

The rest of that distant evening had been gay and festive, although Robert never knew why his wife was suddenly so relaxed.

Harry himself had been something of a mystery to Casey. Over the next few weeks, before the Stevenses' departure for Alaska, they had gone out with Harry several times. He always brought a different woman.

Robert had told her that Harry always kept a stable of three or four girlfriends, all glamorous actresses or debutantes, gorgeous and young, none of them knowing the existence of the others. Harry had once told Robert good-naturedly that Valentine's Day and New Year's Eve were the two worst nights of the year because no woman ever believed him when he said he had to work late and no woman ever forgave him for not being there for those two days.

And yet, Harry had told both Casey and Robert that he desperately wanted to marry—of course, he had to find that right woman, the "perfect" woman. The list of essential attributes of that perfect woman, Robert had explained to Casey, was endless, but five characteristics were essential, and all decidedly placed Casey out of any competition.

Blond, tall—at least five-nine, Harry had explained—Swedish-speaking—Harry's mother had been a native Swede—with no academic credentials and no dependents. Oh, and a great cook.

Casey smiled and wondered who Harry would bring to meet her at the airport. She tried to remember, and was certain she had never actually seen Harry without a female escort.

Joseph was asleep, wrapped around the largest of his teddy bears. On his cheeks were the remains of his recent dessert of cherry-vanilla pudding. Casey leaned forward in her seat to pull the blanket around him. He had survived the trip quite well. He hadn't complained when they ascended or descended, though she was sure the changes in air pressure must have hurt his ears.

She pulled her parka around her like a blanket and settled back into her seat. The trip had been lonely; she didn't even have Leon to talk to because he was up in the pilot's seat. She pulled out the book she had been trying to read since they had left Skip's Place, but the letters waved and shifted before her eyes. She felt tiredness overcome her and closed her eyes. Just a minute's sleep, she thought to herself.

When she awoke, she was baffled by the silence. Or near silence. Just a gentle lapping of waves, the distant hum of planes taking off and landing, accompanied by a faintly fishy smell.

She opened her eyes only to be face-to-face with Leon. His eyes were red and had deep, gray circles beneath them. His jaw was covered with a two-day-old stubble. His scent was pungent, but not in an unattractive way.

"We're here," he said. "Just take what's essential for tonight—we can come back tomorrow."

He took from her hand the cold foam cup, half-filled with coffee, which she had been holding. She stood up, letting her leg cramps unwind. She looked out the portal at the skyline, a blur of red, white and blue lights, blinking and swirling against the pastel sunset.

Leon kicked open the cabin door, letting in a rush of chilly, fresh lake air. He jumped down to the concrete.

"I've got to tie in the plane," he said, looking back up at her. "But hurry, wouldja? I'm godawful tired."

Casey gathered Joseph's clothes and diapers, her lecture notes, which were strewn all over the cabin, and shoved everything into her duffel bag. She picked up Joseph, careful not to startle him from his sleep, wrapping him in a warm quilt. He gave her a sleepy, puzzled look, and she hoped he wouldn't start to cry.

"Sorry, didn't mean to wake you," she said quietly, laying him back up on her shoulder. He snuggled into position and fell back to sleep.

"I'll take Joseph if you can hand him to me," Leon said, reaching up to the door from the tarmac.

Casey gently turned Joseph around and passed him to Leon. She dropped her duffel to the ground and jumped, careful to relax her knees, to cushion the jolt of her landing.

"I'll be damned glad to get a hot shower and some sleep," Leon said, stepping back to let her jump down to the cement runway. "Where do you suggest we bunk?"

"Why, she'll stay with me, of course," an unfamiliar voice announced.

Casey stood up from the crouching position she had found herself in when she had dropped from the plane. Turning in the direction Leon was looking, she smiled at the tall, light-haired man with the camel-hair coat and a paper-wrapped bunch of flowers in hand.

Harry! Darling, sweet Harry.

He must have been waiting for hours, Casey thought. And yet, his smile was as relaxed as if he had just come off a tennis court or a polo field. She glanced around the field, wondering if a budding actress or a glamorous flight at-

tendant had accompanied Harry. Casey was almost disappointed to realize Harry was alone.

"Who are you, buddy?" Leon asked, positioning himself by the plane. He put his right hand protectively over
Joseph's head. "Where'd you come from?"

Casey pulled at Leon's arm, anxious that he not antag-
onize her old friend.

"Why, I'm Professor Kramer," Harry said, extending
his right hand to Leon. "I'm a dear friend of Casey, and
of course, of her...uh, late husband."

Leon ignored the offered hand, and Casey brushed Leon
aside.

"Harry, it's so good to see you," she said. "I didn't
recognize you...it's been over a year."

She didn't say what was on the tip of her tongue—that
in the year she had been away, Harry had aged, no longer
looking like a cheerful playboy, but now consigned to appear exactly as what he truly was: a bachelor who had
waited so long for the perfect woman that he had been
passed by.

Harry leaned over and startled her with a kiss on the
cheek, a kiss that seemed to Casey to communicate a wist-
fulness—so different from the ebullient, harmlessly flir-
tatious Harry she had always known.

She blushed, embarrassed at standing between the two
men, well aware of Leon's bristling displeasure.

"Darling, it's so good to see you," Harry murmured,
and pressed the bouquet into her hands. With his hand
free, he pulled a baby rattle from his coat pocket.

"Darling?" Leon asked.

She stopped herself from explaining that Harry called
everybody darling, that it was just his nature. But then she
realized how insulting such a comment might seem to
Harry, as if it were designed to denigrate his mannerisms.

Instead she glared at Leon, hoping that the chastising look would stop his rude behavior.

Harry allowed his eyes to lazily regard Leon, taking in the rumpled shirt, the unkempt hair, the stubbly chin. "I don't believe we've met, old boy," he said. "You are...?"

"Leon Brodie. I'm Casey's flyboy."

"I see," Harry said, linking his arm in Casey's and turning from him. "It was nice to meet you, Mr. Brodie. And now, Casey, why don't we go to my car? Shouldn't you be taking the baby with us?"

"Uh, Harry," Leon prompted.

"Yes?"

"Harry, I'm also the baby's nanny," Leon announced, playfully patting Joseph's diaper-covered bottom and holding him close. "I'm afraid I'll have to stay where the baby stays. I guess that means your house, huh?"

Casey stared up at Leon, unable to fathom the arrogance that had led him to insinuate himself into Harry's hospitality, and well aware of the pleasures Leon was anticipating at his reluctant host's home: a hot shower, a relaxing dinner, a restful night's sleep. She understood his expectations because they were her own hopes after the long flight.

Harry responded to the cocky glint in Leon's eye with a calm, benevolent smile. He handed Leon the baby rattle he had so thoughtfully brought as a welcoming gift for Joseph.

"Well, of course, and I'm glad you will be joining us because I have arranged for the trustees of the university's museum to dine with Casey this evening, and the baby will need his nanny's care. I suspect you can care for Joseph both when Casey rests before dinner and then when we are away."

Casey could barely suppress a giggle at the sudden panic in Leon's eyes as he looked down at the baby in his hands. She was sure that baby-sitting Joseph had been the furthest thing from Leon Brodie's mind.

Visions of a screaming baby, of endlessly wet diapers, of cleaning rejected pureed foods from every kitchen surface were clearly occupying Leon's thoughts.

"I'll be glad to oblige," he said at last, rather slowly.

Leon's face had flushed and his jaws clenched as he said each labored word, as he considered the enormity of his impending responsibilities. Casey might have sympathized with him, but she was distracted by a new set of images: a hot bath, clean and pressed clothes and the excitement of a meeting with the trustees. These notions appealed to her so much that she put off her impulse to take Leon aside and tell him he couldn't possibly take care of her baby—he just wasn't qualified!

"Here, I'll carry Joseph," she said, pressing the flowers into Harry's arms and reaching out to her son.

"Good," Harry said. "I'll carry the flowers, you carry the baby and Leon will carry your bag."

Harry linked his arm in Casey's free arm and led her toward the lighted parking lot, leaving Leon to scramble to secure the plane for the night, then rush to catch up with them. As Casey and Harry left the runway and reached Harry's jaunty yellow Mercedes, Leon just managed to overtake them, puffing hard as he carried his and Casey's duffels.

Chapter Eight

"Damn!" Leon muttered, not for the first time that evening.

His glass had toppled and beer was quickly spreading out along the table. Leon hoisted a howling Joseph up over his shoulder. He could see his reflection in the mirror behind the counter of the small neighborhood coffee shop. Somehow he didn't look like the suave, debonair Leon Brodie he was used to seeing, or at least like the suave, debonair Leon Brodie he was once able to pretend he was.

Instead there was a guy with a two-day-old stubble and a baby who didn't stop crying for a second. A guy with bits of banana and dried baby formula stuck to his hair, put there by a certain someone. A guy whose shirt had baby spit-up that was destined to never come out. A guy who hadn't slept for nearly forty-eight hours—and looked it.

Joseph shrieked and wiggled. Leon felt the disapproving stares of several patrons in the small coffee shop. He smiled foolishly at a gaggle of yuppie types who seemed particularly disturbed by Joseph, hoping that his look communicated an apology.

"It's my first baby," he explained, and the group nodded in tandem and returned to their conversation.

"Probably comparing BMWs," Leon muttered to Joseph.

The waitress, a tall, blond, girl-next-door type wearing a Chicago Bears T-shirt, flung a towel onto Leon's table.

"This is the third beer he's spilled," she said, amiably sopping up the spilled beer. "At this rate, you'll have a twenty-dollar check and I don't think you've even gotten a chance to have a single sip."

Joseph whooped and wriggled some more in Leon's arms, and he kicked the stuffed squirrel Leon had ferreted out of Casey's duffel. The toy rolled across the bar, down on the floor, coming to rest under the table next to their booth.

Leon shrugged. Lost—that squirrel might as well have fallen into the Chicago River—after all, how could he hang on to the squirming Joseph and reach down to the floor at the same time?

Leon pulled Harry's blue-and-red rattle from his shirt pocket and waved it in front of the baby's face. Joseph turned and grabbed it. He shoved it into his mouth and slurped at it contentedly. For a second, Leon had the relief of a quiet, stationary Joseph.

It had seemed like such a good idea, coming to the tiny restaurant across the street from Harry's brownstone. After Casey and Harry had left, Joseph had been inconsolable, turning his lower lip inside out and crying even when Leon, in rotating order, sang "Twinkle, Twinkle Little Star" at the top of his lungs, played the Rolling Stones on the radio, offered formula and banana, and imitated each animal he remembered from the Alabama farm where he had grown up. In fact, the only distraction that had pleased Joseph had been a game of airplane—in which Leon balanced Joseph on his head and ran through the house bellowing like a 747—and that game had ended when Joseph cheerfully, with a most charming smile on his face, regurgitated his dinner on Leon's head.

Dinner had been bananas and cereal, which his mother, Casey, had fed him after she had showered, napped and dressed—dressed in a lace-trimmed burgundy velvet dress that was somehow demure and yet provocatively sensual at the same time. She wore subtle perfume that reminded Leon of violets.

As he was wrestling with a baby, she was out at some fancy restaurant, dining with fancy trustees while he couldn't even get a sip of a beer or eat a simple hot dog.

Leon's temperature rose as he wondered if, as she most likely talked with these strangers about a dozen academic topics that he had never heard or cared about, she measured his manhood on the basis of some scholarly test that he could never pass.

The waitress interrupted Leon's dark thoughts, putting down yet another beer in front of Leon, who was still struggling to maintain his hold on Joseph. He took a quick gulp of the drink.

It was hard being out in public with a baby, he thought, mentally determined to always sympathize, maybe even offer help to, any parents he encountered in similar straits.

To think that he had been the one to tell Casey and that professor that he was able to baby-sit Joseph while they went to dinner.

And when Casey gave him instructions—what to feed Joseph, when to diaper him, how to put him down for the night—he hadn't been able to concentrate because of her perfume. Something light and flowery and feminine—violets fresh from the field on a summer day.

"What are you wearing?" he had asked.

"What do you mean?" She was puzzled at what had prompted the question.

"Your perfume?" Leon smiled mischievously.

"Nothing," she said innocently. "It's just me."

The answer was enough to put him over the edge. He felt dizzy with hunger for her. And her chattering like a magpie about emergency phone numbers and what to do if Joseph spit up.

Now he wished he had paid attention more, because it was starting to look as if he'd have to go back to Kramer's house and play airplane again. Although Joseph was as happy as a clam in the restaurant, he was hard to contain.

He had wanted to just hand the baby to that sanctimonious professor and grab her in his arms right then and there.

Instead, he had lied. "Oh, Casey, for crying out loud, it's not like I haven't taken care of a baby before."

And she had looked puzzled, perhaps remembering the disastrous feeding in Skip's kitchen. Why shouldn't she? He just wanted her out of the house before he did something foolish.

At least Casey and Harry got to eat. Leon had ordered a hot dog, and Joseph had grabbed it out of his hands. And then had dropped it to the floor, laughing and smiling as if it was the funniest thing in the world. Things had gone downhill from there.

"How old is he?" the waitress asked.

"Oh, he's uh, six months," Leon answered, aware that the waitress was staring at Joseph. "Yeah, six months."

"He's so darling," she said dreamily. She returned Joseph's grin with a brilliant smile of her own. "You really are a cutey! How many teeth does he have?'' she asked, reluctantly turning her attention to Leon.

"Teeth?'' Leon looked at Joseph, who was busily sucking the rattle and staring across Leon's face toward something in the distance. Leon followed Joseph's gaze right to the face of an even more stunning blonde seated at the window. She was smiling and wiggling her finger at Joseph.

"I'm not sure—twelve?''

"That's an awful lot for his age. My nephew is eighteen months and he only has six.'' She looked at Leon disbelievingly.

"Well, maybe it's not quite twelve. Four.'' His eyes wandered to the blonde who was now staring at him intently. "I'm not sure, they come in so fast. But there's a lot.'' Joseph dropped his rattle onto the bar, and reached for Leon's drink. Leon scrambled to pull him back.

"The kid is strong. You look like you could use some help,'' the waitress said. "You want me to hold the baby while you drink some of your beer—maybe even eat your hot dog? I can hold him until another customer needs me.''

She saw his hesitation.

"I'll take him in the kitchen, and I promise to leave the door open so you can see us every second,'' she said.

"You read my mind. I'm sorry,'' Leon told her. "It's just, these days, you can't be too careful.''

"Oh, don't worry, I'm not offended. I'd feel the same way about my own baby.''

They shared a brief, trusting smile and Leon lifted Joseph up over the hardwood table. It was such a relief just to be able to relax! The waitress expertly rested the baby on one hip and jostled him up and down. Joseph grabbed for her hair, staring into her eyes like a regular Don Juan. His eyebrows even moved up and down in a suggestive way that Leon himself had perfected only after exhaustive practice in front of the mirror when he was a teenager.

This boy's got a way with the ladies, Leon admitted.

"He's so cute," the little Casanova's romantic conquest gushed. "I forgot to ask—what's his name?"

"Joseph," Leon answered, raising his glass to his lips.

"Well, Joseph," she purred, turning her attention exclusively to her charge, "how about taking a tour of the kitchen with me?"

In ecstasy over the feminine attention he was receiving, Joseph was happy to be transported out of the dining room. The waitress carefully propped open the swinging doors to the kitchen and Leon relaxed.

Leon slumped into his seat, allowing his exhaustion—two days traveling—to overcome him. Still listening to the banter between the waitress and Joseph, he closed his eyes, and was surprised when he opened them.

The blonde from the window seat was now right up next to him; he could smell the heavy scent of roses drowning out the coffee, cookies and hot dog smell of the coffee shop. She slid into the seat opposite his and he felt her silky stockings brush against his jeans.

"Hard to get any time to yourself with a baby, isn't it?" she asked breathlessly.

Immediately he realized that there was something odd going on.

He didn't feel anything when she talked, no sense of challenge or adventure. A few months ago, a blonde getting within fifty feet of him was enough to send his hormones into overdrive. And now? Maybe it was simply because she wasn't what he had thought; the strikingly beautiful face he had seen from several feet away had, upon closer inspection, turned out to be a rather hardened, heavily made-up one.

"Yeah, he's a real pistol out in public," he said, feeling vaguely disloyal to Joseph, as if Joseph, who was happily eating a maraschino cherry in the kitchen, could care what Leon was saying about him. "Yeah, Joseph's really a handful," he finished.

"My name's Grace," the blonde mewed. "Mind if I join you?"

"Sure, go ahead, sit right down."

He gestured at the seat she already occupied.

"Name's Leon," he said. They nodded at each other. Up close, he recognized thick black lines accentuating her eyes, and her lipstick, the color of a stop sign. The rose perfume seemed a little strong. Maybe it had just been too long since he had smelled any perfume at all. She seemed a little older than when she had been a few yards out of reach. He felt bad about being so critical.

He sat silently, as she—somehow sensing his resistance—continued the conversation. But perhaps she took his drooping eyes as a sign of interest. Or maybe his unblinking stare, focused unseeingly at a point on the table just in front of her lacquered nails.

In fact, his tired eyes were so unseeing that he didn't notice the door to the shop opening, didn't hear the cheerful bell announcing a new customer, didn't feel a thing until a tiny, angry fist pounded on the table, jolting him and his sensual companion to attention.

"Where is my baby?" Casey, towering over him, screamed. "Where is my baby?"

Leon was so tired that he utterly forgot Joseph was safely in the arms of the waitress—within view, for that matter. He startled and looked around for a scant moment, forgetting that Joseph was not even twenty feet from him. Customers stared in censorious amazement, and conversations dropped into dead silence.

Grace stared up at the madwoman.

"It's been wonderful talking with you, Leon," she murmured, as she slid from her seat.

"I leave you for one minute with my baby and you run off with some, some..." Casey, wide-eyed, searched for the words to describe his tablemate, and, for a brief second as Grace negotiated her exit, the two women stared each other down, until Grace slunk out the door to the sidewalk.

"I'm sorry, Casey," Leon said, shaking his sleepy head of its cobwebs. "Joseph is just fine, he's—"

"You couldn't wait for Harry and me to leave so you could run off to get yourself the kind of woman you seem to do best with! It's only luck that when I couldn't find you at Harry's, I came over here!"

He threw a twenty-dollar bill on the table, knowing that whatever was coming next wouldn't leave a lot of time to calculate the proper tip. Then he stood up, ready to take Casey to Joseph, ready to listen to the scolding that was most assuredly not going to be over anytime soon.

With animal-like strength born of concern and rage over her son, Casey shoved him back into his seat.

"Just tell me where he is," she commanded.

"Back there," he said lamely.

With a brief but cutting glare, she turned heel and ran toward the kitchen door, with twenty silent customers turning to stare as she passed. The waitress, with Joseph safely cradled in her arms, stood silently waiting for Casey to take her baby.

"Mama, Mama," Joseph squealed and fell into Casey's arms.

"Oh, thank God you're safe!" Casey wailed, and held her baby tightly. She smiled forgivingly at the waitress, murmured her thanks, and—self-conscious with all the attention the domestic drama had generated—rushed from the coffee shop.

Now the customers, sensing the finale to the tableau laid out for their entertainment, turned their attention to Leon. He stood, and with a quick nod to the baffled waitress, followed Casey out of the shop.

She stood on the sidewalk, holding Joseph close to her chest, gratefully inhaling the fresh-bread smell of his hair. How wonderful it was to find him safe and secure!

She started to walk, turning not toward the three-story brownstone that Harry called home, but along the commercial street—lit with fluorescentlike sodium street lamps and bustling with Saturday nightlife. While in Alaska she could walk late at night on a deserted, calming footpath, but here in Chicago, the best she could hope for was a crowded sidewalk. It was disturbing, and somehow didn't lead to the calmness she sought, but the crowded city was something she was simply going to have to adjust to.

She heard Leon's feet pounding the cement pavement as he caught up with her at the intersection, and for a full block she refused to acknowledge him as he kept pace with her. At last, irritated with him, she stopped.

"Why are you following me? Why don't you run off with one of your blondes?"

"You can't walk on a street this late at night by yourself," Leon explained, in what seemed to her to be a particularly patronizing tone. "Especially when you have Joseph's safety to consider."

She decided to not challenge him, but instead turned toward her self-made path, reluctantly accepting his jacket, which he draped around her shoulders to fend off the September chill.

"Look, you would have done the same thing," Leon explained, surprised at how quickly he had to walk to keep up with her. "I looked into Harry's refrigerator and the only things he had were vitamins and a case of champagne. I didn't feel like eating bananas and baby cereal for dinner—and besides, I was getting a little stir-crazy with Joseph in the house. You're back almost two hours early—how was I supposed to know?"

"What about handing him over to a total stranger?" Casey threw over her shoulder. "What about the blonde?"

"I couldn't eat my dinner," Leon said. "Haven't you ever let a waitress hold him while you put a few bites into your mouth?"

Not only a waitress, but every salesclerk, bank teller and gas-station attendant that she had let hold Joseph while she ate, fumbled with her checkbook or went to the bathroom loomed in front of her. *A vengeful God is going to make all those helpful people never lift a finger on Joseph's behalf again if I don't forgive Leon,* she thought.

"All right, but what about the blonde?" she demanded, desperately trying to maintain her indignant tone. "You're out there picking up women and my son is . . ."

He yanked her shoulder, pulling her back from the curb just as a devilish left-turning convertible glided over where she would have been. For a moment, shocked at the close call, the two stared at the speeding car as it disappeared into the traffic.

With a barest shrug of thanks, Casey looked up at Leon, waiting for an explanation.

"She sat down next to me—I didn't invite her," Leon said, shrugging defensively. "Besides, she's not my type."

"I thought your type was blond and willing—and she looked like it."

"That's not my type."

"Well, just what is your type?"

Their eyes locked and instantly both knew that to answer the question, Leon would open raw emotional possibilities that neither could face. Each considered the chances, chances that could be forecast by a few simple words, and each backed away—Casey considering a man who could only pull her back to a life she had rejected, Leon considering a woman who could only drag him into a future that he wasn't ready for.

The light changed. Casey crossed the street, now not racing from Leon in anger, but walking with Leon at her side. They admired the window displays of the shops and pointed out particularly interesting people as they passed. At a sidewalk hot dog stand, Leon at last bought his dinner and wolfed it down, buying a cola to share with Casey.

"Why did you come back so early?" he asked.

Casey shook her head, thinking of the dinner. Thinking of what it was that had made her leave at the earliest moment, pleading jet lag. How could she explain—especially when a dinner like the one tonight was exactly what she had been looking forward to for months? How could she explain how bored and lonely she had been, listening to the snooty society ladies' gossip and the sonorous speeches from the Trustees' president? She had, she confessed only to herself, longed for Skip's incessant piano playing and toast making, or an Athabascan villagers' feast complete with storytelling and joviality.

Joseph shifted in her arms, happily watching every new diversion on the street, and she remembered part of what had made her give her excuses.

"I missed you," she whispered into the soft, auburn hair of her son.

"I'm flattered," Leon said, gently putting his arm into the crook of hers created by her grip on Joseph.

"I was talking to Joseph," she answered, barely suppressing a giggle.

After a split second of embarrassment at the way he had trapped himself, Leon joined her relaxed laughter.

Casey gently placed Joseph into his crib, which had been placed in the hallway outside of Harry's guest room. She pulled the soft quilt around his shoulders and shifted his arms into a comfortable position. She stared at her son, wistfully hoping for a sleep like his, a sleep untroubled by doubt and fear.

Had she made a mistake, tying her future to the exhibit, to the university, to the city? If tonight was any indication, it was going to take a long time before she was comfortable with her choices. The crush of unfamiliar people, the pretentious conversations, the jittery anxiety that accompanied being locked in a cement-and-steel closet with five million other people.

Although she certainly would never admit it to Leon, the most enjoyable part of the evening had come after she had made her excuses to Harry—who barely noticed, caught up as he was in conversation—and had finished an evening walk with Leon and Joseph. They had bought ice-cream cones and when Leon had asked if he could watch television in her bedroom—the only television in Harry's house—while she gave Joseph his bath, she hadn't hesitated in saying yes.

Somehow the sounds of the evening news and Leon's occasional one-sided conversations with the anchors had been a soothing accompaniment to the task of cleaning Joseph.

I should tell Leon that he's a good nanny, she thought, smiling at the memory of the confrontation at the coffee shop.

But when she entered the brightly lit guest room, she was surprised to find Leon sprawled on the bed, sound asleep. She turned off the television and approached him.

"Leon, wake up," she whispered, shaking him gently.

He murmured a reply, but didn't open his eyes, and within seconds Casey heard the rhythmic breathing of a deep sleep. Stern words, more jostling and turning the nightstand lamp on and off a few times did nothing to change his condition. *And who could blame the guy?* Casey thought, remembering that Leon had not slept in more than forty-eight hours.

She considered her choices, knowing that moving Leon off the chintz-covered bed was not one of them. She could sleep in the room that Harry had set aside for Leon, but that room was in the basement, and Casey was concerned about not hearing Joseph if he were to wake in the middle of the night. And, given Leon's condition, it looked as if Joseph's nanny wasn't going to hear Joseph's cries, either.

She could sleep in Harry's room, but it seemed a bit presumptuous to rely on his hospitality and then extend it to his own bed. Besides, he wasn't home to ask and what would he think of her if he came home and found her asleep in his bed? For a brief second, she wondered whether Harry had ever been attracted to her. She decided not, because she had none of the feminine qualities that Harry deemed important. On the other hand, it wouldn't do to be in his bed. What if he thought he was being obligated to accept an invitation from her?

That left one possibility.

Changing into a flannel shirt, she turned out the lights and got into bed.

I'm never going to get to sleep, she thought . . . just before she nodded off.

Chapter Nine

She couldn't remember the dream when she woke, but she certainly knew what it had been about: she still felt the sizzling ache in her belly and the restless shifting of her legs. A soft, catlike purr settled in her throat as she luxuriated in the feeling of the body that rubbed up against her back. Buses roared along the street outside, accompanied by the gentle peeping of resident pigeons. When she opened her eyes, she found herself face-to-face with a sun-drenched pink and blue papered section of wall. Without even moving she knew exactly where she was.

And who she was with!

It wasn't so bad to be attracted to Leon, she thought to herself as she closed her eyes again—attracted in a purely physical manner. In fact, society could not survive if every twenty-four-year-old woman were a cold fish, Casey considered, with her cool, calm, cultural anthropologist hat firmly on her head. And if it weren't for the female sexual response, women would have no incentive to engage in relations with men like Leon.

It was difficult to remain objective about this when his fingers were gently tapping on her back!

Would it be so horrible to. . . well, to get involved with him? She certainly wasn't thinking about tying her future to him, or ruining her chances of becoming associated with the university, or of living in Chicago. Just a physical relationship. Would it be so horrible to discover that the sexual problems with her late husband had not simply been because she was abnormal in some way?

The tapping was becoming more insistent, and she realized that some decisions were purely emotional or physical or spiritual or something—just not as coolly rational as she would like.

"Leon," she whispered, as she determined to give herself to the hot rush of passion. "Leon."

She rolled over and found herself face-to-face with a bare-chested Leon lounging in bed, propped up on one elbow, smiling knowingly.

Joseph lay between them, his feet in his hands, a broad smile on his face, his hands still tapping her.

Casey bolted upright.

"Sorry we woke you—we were playing with our feet," Leon explained, knowing damn well the reason for the look of horror on Casey's face. "Well, really just his feet—mine are too big and I wouldn't be very comfortable in his position."

The sight of the two males lying in her bed was as effective as the proverbial cold shower. But while the activity that had been uppermost in her mind—and body—a few moments before was now impossible, Casey couldn't really stay disappointed long. She smiled happily and kissed each of the toes Joseph presented.

"He woke up about an hour ago," Leon continued. "I brought him in here because he wanted his mommy. He was very content once he realized he was next to you."

"You're a good nanny," Casey told him, snuggling into the sheets next to her baby.

"You didn't think so last night."

"Last night was different."

"And this morning, you feel better about me in so many ways?" he asked, pausing to let the words carry a subtle ambiguity.

Casey blushed, hoping that her momentary lapse of reserve hadn't been too apparent. When Leon's questioning stare made her too uncomfortable, she sat up again, looking for the excuse to stop this ridiculous conversation.

And this ridiculous physical proximity!

"Leon, it's already nine o'clock," she gasped as she noticed the nightstand clock out of the corner of her eye. "I have to look over my notes and be ready for an interview with the university alumni magazine at eleven and for a luncheon at twelve. How could you have let me sleep so late?"

She jumped from the bed and looked around the room, trying to remember where she had put her clothes. And her shoes. And her bathrobe. And where were the lecture notes? And did she have a clean pair of stockings without a run?

An annoying, appreciative wolf whistle stopped her reverie. Joseph tried to imitate the sound, and he wriggled to sit up. Casey followed Leon's eyes to the source of his juvenile pleasure.

The oversize men's shirt that she had pilfered from Harry's closet barely covered the pink lace border of her panties and her naked legs suddenly seemed way too long, utterly out of proportion with the rest of her body.

Joseph tried another wolf whistle, and was proud of his two-tone shriek.

"Leon, your mind is always in the gutter," she said primly, grabbing an oversize plaid men's robe from the closet.

"Oh, and not in the world of the intellect like all your fancy friends?" He jumped from the bed, determined to argue, his anger over the course of their relationship in the past week overflowing. All he succeeded in doing was drawing her attention to his own body—a perfect, masculine triangle of muscle. "Is it that you think I'm stupid because I don't have a string of letters after my name and a fancy title?"

"Not stupid, just not educated."

Joseph tried the wolf whistle again.

"And education is all that matters, huh? Without a degree I can't even get to first base with you, isn't that right?"

"You just can't offer me the kind of relationship I would want," Casey explained, uncomfortable at the sight of him. At the nearness of him. "I want security and love and respect and..."

"And you want things to be dull," Leon countered. "You don't have any room in there for this."

He stepped forward and pulled her into his arms, his mouth on hers, kissing her the way she had once anticipated, had once imagined... had dreamed about not even a few minutes ago.

And all her reluctance seemed like shifting sand—difficult to hold on to, impossible to keep.

Joseph erupted in a peal of wolf whistles, laughter and baby shrieks. Casey jerked away from the embrace.

"Don't do that in front of my baby again," she warned.

"He's mine, too," Leon countered, releasing her and putting on a pair of jeans that had been discarded on the floor sometime during the night.

Baffled by his comment, Casey stared at him.

"I'm his nanny, remember?" Leon picked up Joseph who, Casey noted with a twinge of jealousy, fairly leaped into his arms. "Come on, Joseph, let's go downstairs."

The two males left Casey standing alone in the middle of the room. Just before they reached the stairs, she caught up with them.

"Would you marry me?" she asked Leon.

He stopped at the top of the stairs, and Casey was pleased to see the frisson of fear that overcame him. He swallowed hard, his Adam's apple bobbing.

"Was that a proposal?"

"No, actually, it was a hypothetical," Casey said, proud that she had placed him on the defensive. "I know you are incapable of pledging yourself to a woman and I'm simply telling you that without that sort of possibility I wouldn't enter into a sexual liaison with anyone. And ninety-five percent of the women in this society would feel the same."

For a few moments he appeared stumped by her comment. Then a slow, wicked smile passed over his face.

"Yeah, but if my partner here hadn't been in bed with us this morning, I think you would have," he said. "Oh, and I think ninety-five percent of the female population would, too."

And, without even a glance at her, he stalked down the stairs.

She avoided him for the rest of the morning, reading in the kitchen while he and Joseph watched *Sesame Street* in the living room, ironing a blouse in the dining room when they went to the kitchen for breakfast. She wasn't sure exactly why, but in the battle of the sexes, she felt she had let down the team a little.

Harry came home from teaching an early-morning seminar at ten-thirty. With a hasty goodbye to Joseph, Casey gathered up her notes and quickly patted her hair into place. She was glad Harry was driving her to her appointments; she hadn't seen him since she had left the dinner the night before.

"You missed a great dessert," Harry chided her playfully as he expertly steered the car onto the crowded Lake Shore Drive. "And the announcement that Mrs. Paley—she was the old lady seated on my right—would be giving the university a cool million for its endowment campaign."

"And I missed your latest conquest, I'm sure." Casey smiled.

"What's that supposed to mean?"

"Wasn't there a blonde, very young—the one wearing a pink dress?"

He thought for a moment, and then frowned with mock indignation.

"That was the new chairman of the North American Archaeology department," he explained, his voice filled with a bitter tone that made Casey think she shouldn't have teased him.

Had Harry changed? He had, after all, arrived at the airport alone, with no blond tennis pro or aspiring model on his arm. In fact, she hadn't seen any women in his orbit. What was wrong with Harry?

"I've stopped looking for the perfect woman," he said suddenly, his eyes sharply concentrating on the road even as he seemed to be intently reading her mind. "I've utterly stopped looking."

"Does that mean you don't want to get married any-more?" Casey asked, genuinely surprised. "What about the tall, blond, Swedish-speaking woman with no dependents?"

He grimaced and appeared absorbed by the problems of negotiating the exit off Lake Shore Drive into the busy Loop area—the six or seven blocks of busiest commercial real estate in Chicago, bound by the "loop" of commuter train tracks.

"I've always had a list of qualities that the 'perfect' woman has," he said as they stopped at a red light. "I've told anyone and everyone that I want very much to get married—but it has to be perfect. Well, I finally realized that I had probably dated every woman in Chicago that fits the general description of what I think is the perfect woman—and a lot of women who don't."

"And?"

"And I've decided that I'm going to sit back and let love happen to me instead of trying to go out there and grab it," Harry said. "If I fall in love with a gray-haired lady with fourteen kids who doesn't speak Swedish or even English—so be it. I will fall in love with whomever God or fate or nature or whatever's in charge decides."

They sat silently as he pulled the car into the four-story parking garage. Casey was surprised and disheartened by how the tall buildings shielded the inner Loop from light, making the city seem dark gray even on this, the brightest of sunny days.

Suddenly she thought of Robert, of the type of love that he had had for her. Was it a calculated kind, born of a list of preconceived qualities? Had he had a list like Harry's, but simply one that she had fit into? Had his love for her been like an unexpected dictate from the heavens, a surprise, an enchanted gift? Or something a little less romantic?

"Harry, tell me about Robert," she said as they left the car and headed for the building where she would be interviewed. "I know he thought of you as a brother...as his closest friend. What was he like?"

Harry stopped his fast gait and stared at her.

"You don't know the answer to that?"

She shook her head. "I remember things and I think that maybe I'm remembering the Robert that was real," she said, hesitantly putting into words what she had never even allowed herself to think before. "But then I think that I'm not remembering the real Robert. I'm just fantasizing about a man that I wanted to love."

"And why is it so important for you to know the difference?"

"Because if he was like the Robert I fantasize about, then I feel guilty because I didn't treat him...because I didn't—" her face flushed with red-hot embarrassment "—I didn't respond to him the way I think a wife should, and I'm ashamed because I think I have those feelings..." She decided to stop, unwilling to share with him the not fully acknowledged feelings she had for Leon.

"But if it's not the real Robert you're remembering?"

"Then, I'm not tormented in quite the same way," she said softly.

He pulled her to a bench up against the elevators leading out of the parking garage. They sat down and she waited patiently for him to gather his thoughts.

"Robert was a remarkable anthropologist," he said. "He was able to move into a new culture and make observations that were completely objective, with none of his own thoughts and feelings layered over his work. His only flaw was that he was sometimes incapable of seeing the extraordinary emotional power of some personal interactions within a culture."

"I wasn't talking about him as an anthropologist," Casey chided softly.

"But I am talking about him as a human being."

They sat quietly, listening to the cacophony of late-morning traffic in one of the busiest cities in the country.

"When he decided he was going to marry," Harry continued, speaking almost as if she were not near him, "he decided on a set of qualities that any woman he considered would have to have. Clearly, she had to be in his field, ready to transfer, capable of good work, and beautiful to boot—Robert had done enough fieldwork to decide that beauty in women was a very important trait."

"That listing of qualifications sounds like what you do," Casey said, and then added, "or what you did."

"There's a difference, I suppose. I always waited to see if I fell in love with a woman with the right qualities but Robert just went out and married her, actually you, telling himself that he would love you as soon as you were wed." Harry fell silent and then, seeing the look of horror on Casey's face, added, "Of course, he did fall in love with you—in the way that Robert could."

"But after we were married, he seldom told me that he loved me," Casey muttered, the shock over Harry's words beginning to color her thinking.

"It wouldn't dawn on Robert to say something like that," Harry said. "You should understand that, whatever you got out of that marriage, Robert got a lot more."

Casey thought she was going to cry, as the assumptions of her marriage were gently destroyed by a few simple, well-intentioned words from Robert's closest friend. But everything Harry had said meshed with the things she had observed about her husband and the things Skip had told her.

Could it be that when she had "failed" in her sexual response to Robert, it had been a valid reaction to the fact that her marriage had been based, not so much on love, as upon mutual convenience or upon mutual needs that had been, in true academic fashion, cataloged in some orderly system?

Sensing the tumultuous feelings Casey was experiencing, Harry took her hand.

"We have an interviewer upstairs who wants to get started," he said gently. "Robert was my dearest friend, and he was a wonderful husband to you, I'm sure. But we have to continue."

She looked up at Harry in surprise. Couldn't he understand that this entire exhibit—perhaps even her desire to live in Chicago and work at the university—all of her actions seemed designed to go back into the past, to reclaim a Robert who perhaps had never existed?

Without another word, she followed him to the interviewer's office.

The interview went very well; Casey felt that, with each question about their work, Robert's stature increased. Robert was an extraordinary anthropologist, she reminded herself. What she didn't notice was how her own reputation was evolving.

Casey and Harry seemed to have made a secret, silent pact—one that simply required them to pretend that they had never spoken about Robert in such intimate terms. So, cheerfully, perhaps even too cheerfully to be entirely natural, they drove to the university campus for a luncheon with the entire anthropology department. Casey was relieved and happy when she was invited to join the faculty as a guest lecturer for the coming semester; such a position would surely lead to a permanent offer to stay.

Her life was so secure, and her future seemed to fall into place like so many pieces of a jigsaw puzzle.

When they arrived home, exhausted and victorious over the day's events, Harry and Casey found Joseph and his nanny vigorously cheering at a football game on television.

"Mama, Mama," Joseph cried when he saw her enter the front door. Game forgotten, he carefully rolled off the living-room couch and crawled over to her.

"Come here, little boy," she coaxed and pulled him into her arms.

"What an extraordinary example of male bonding," Harry said, smiling benevolently at the television screen as he passed into the kitchen.

Leon hit the remote control button and the picture dissolved.

"And here I just thought we were watching a game together," he drawled.

Casey could sense the undercurrents of anger and wounded pride that Leon's voice carried. But she was so tired and happy to be home with her son that she decided it was better to ignore him.

"I'm going to take a nap with Joseph," she said and fled upstairs.

Harry reappeared in the living room with two bottles of beer. "Here, I understand you like beer, so I bought some on my way home from the dinner last night," he said, and handed one to Leon.

Leon didn't want to drink so early in the day, but didn't want to appear impolite, so he took a quick sip of his beer and nodded his appreciation to Harry. Taking this smile as a sign of friendship, Harry sat on the chair opposite the couch and took a similar, tentative sip of his beer. The grimace on Harry's face told Leon everything he needed to know about him.

Harry didn't like beer.

"Thanks," Leon said, holding his bottle aloft.

"No problem," Harry said, with a forced casualness in his tone.

The two men sat silently for minutes, uncomfortable, uncertain of what to say to each other. They simultaneously took another unwanted sip of their beers, and then Harry ventured into unknown territory.

"If you want to finish watching the game, I would be happy to watch with you," he said, pushing his chair in front of the television.

Leon pressed the remote control button and the game, midway through its first quarter, continued.

After a few minutes, Harry leaned over to Leon conspiratorially. "I hope you won't mind my asking you, but could you explain the game to me? I've never watched football before."

Leon stared at Harry in amazement. He had never seen a man Harry's age—must be in his fifties, he guessed—who didn't understand football. The man must be crazy, the same kind of intellectual snob that Casey seemed to be. He reluctantly moved over on the couch and motioned Harry to join him.

"First, I have to explain the field," he said, using the commercial break for a quick lecture. He turned a coffee-table book over on its back for a surface and explained punts, goals, yardage and touchdowns. Harry watched with utter and complete concentration.

By the time the second quarter began, Harry was a confirmed Chicago Bears fan.

And he and Leon were friends.

Chapter Ten

With Joseph in his car seat, the three adults drove to the Water Tower Mall, a glass-and-marble confection of a building that housed some of the trendiest shops in the city, as well as some of the standbys—department stores nearly as old as Chicago itself. Harry had been absolutely right when he had suggested that Casey purchase a suit for the day of the lecture; it just wouldn't do for her to show up in either her "good" velvet dress or the remaining items of her wardrobe: long underwear, flannel shirts and jeans.

Casey picked out a box of frango mints at Marshall Field's and, although she couldn't explain why, she declined the clerk's offer to ship the mints to Skip in Alaska.

"No, thanks, I'll post them myself," Casey said, convincing herself that since there were so many things she would be mailing back to Skip, she better hang on to the box.

They went to a women's boutique and Casey bought a red suit with gold buttons to wear to the lecture plus an extra black skirt and a few tops. With these in hand, she knew she could get through a fast-paced week of museum-related parties and interviews.

"Now I have to pick up a suit for tomorrow's lecture," Leon announced as they left the store. He carried Casey's shopping bag, while Joseph remained quiet in Harry's arms.

Casey was baffled. She had never thought Leon would want to go to the lecture and he had even surprised her when he had told her that he wanted to go shopping with her and Harry. She had come downstairs to find the two men utterly captivated by the football game. In fact, Harry had been whooping with delight over a particular play.

What was going on with these men? Harry was turning into a lunatic football fan and Leon was turning into a man of letters.

She stopped herself from telling Leon that the lecture was going to be boring—boring to someone outside the field. Any way that she put it would sound conceited and rude. But she wondered if he would have any interest in the series of slides and the hour-long talk on research methodology, Athabascan culture and mythology. Casey was starting to think it was possible that such a talk was—quite simply—boring to anyone, even a seasoned and devoted anthropologist. Wasn't it a lot more fun and interesting to stay in the field and do the work than it was to talk about it? They went up the escalator to a fashionable men's store.

"What do you think of this one?" Harry said, pointing to a store window mannequin wearing a gray suit of Italian design.

"Perfect," Leon agreed and went into the store.

Casey sat at a chair in front of a row of suits, curious to see what Leon would look like in a suit. Harry wandered around the store with Joseph in his arms, the two males fingering silk ties and admiring broadcloth shirts.

"Oh, wow," Casey heard a female voice exclaim and she turned around to see a shop girl pointing at a customer. Casey looked toward the dressing-room mirror.

It was Leon, looking so magnificent in his new suit that she was flabbergasted. The gray brushed silk encased his shoulders and skimmed his trunk. The brilliant white shirt accentuated the rugged flush of his skin. And the turquoise silk of his tie drew the observer to wonder at his green eyes. He truly looks as if he were born to wear nice suits, Casey thought, her eyes critically appraising him.

Suddenly Casey found it difficult to suppress a laugh. Leon stopped his turn in front of the mirror.

"What's so funny?" he asked, his eyes narrowing defensively.

Casey pointed at his bare feet.

He looked down and relaxed, smiling at her good-naturedly.

"I guess I need some shoes, too," he said. "Maybe while they're altering the suit, we can find some."

Her smile softened, and she found herself again admiring him. She had thought that he was so rough-hewn that he wouldn't look right in a suit and tie.

Boy, was she wrong.

And surprised. It was intriguing how Leon always had something new about him, something that surprised her, some way that she learned another thing that made him worth admiring.

Like coming back to take her to Chicago. Like being friends with every airport manager and fill-up kid across the country. Like taking care of Joseph. Like becoming friends with Harry—Harry, who had understandably been quite leery of him.

"You like the suit," Leon interrupted, standing over her.

"Yes, you look wonderful," she said.

"I want to make sure that I can be someone you're not ashamed to be seen with," he said softly.

"Why would I be ashamed?" She instantly felt guilty about every time she had brought his lack of education to his attention, every time she had dismissed him in her mind because she thought he didn't measure up.

"You'd be ashamed to know me if I didn't fit in tomorrow," Leon pressed.

"You'll fit in, I'm sure of it." And, looking at him now, she was sure.

After a tailor took his measurements, they bought Leon a pair of shoes. By the time they returned to pick up the altered suit, it was time to go back to Harry's. Joseph played patty cake with Casey in the back seat of the car when they drove back to Harry's Hyde Park home.

"I'm afraid I have one more course to teach," Harry announced as he pulled to a stop in front of the house. "One of those evening courses. I'll be back around ten, ten-thirty."

With a quick goodbye, he was gone and Casey and Leon were left to bring Joseph and the shopping bags into the house. Leon unlocked the front door and turned on the lights.

"Want me to make you some dinner?" he asked. "You can take care of Joseph, keep me company in the kitchen?"

She nodded, and followed him to the back of the house. While he put together hamburgers, she fed Joseph mashed eggs. After only a few moments, she felt uncomfortable when she realized Leon was staring at her, even while the meat sputtered grease.

"We need to talk," Leon said.

"About what?" She looked down at the mashed eggs in front of her.

"I think you shouldn't stay here in Chicago. I think you should return to Alaska—Skip's back there, you have work you can do there." He foundered as he searched for the special explanation that would bring her back. "You can walk outside at night without worrying about getting run over," he finished lamely. "You can't do that here in Chicago."

"I'm staying here, Leon. I was offered a job at the university today, one that I know will turn into a permanent position."

He pulled up a chair next to hers and tousled Joseph's hair. Delighted, Joseph clutched Leon's hand.

"The other reason I'm asking you to come back to Alaska is that I thought we had something special together," he said, staring down at the plate of eggs and toast and looking up at her only after a deep, courage-enhancing breath. "I thought we had it from the moment this little fellow was born."

She stared at him silently, knowing that she had felt the same. Knowing that she had spent many a night after Joseph's birth remembering the tall, dark-haired stranger who had been there with her. Knowing that she had felt too much, far too much, of the turbulent feelings that only the most passionate of kisses could evoke. Knowing that she had hungered for him in a way that she hadn't for her husband—knowing, too, that resolving her feelings about her husband was only possible because of this catalyst.

"You're right," she said softly, putting her hand in his. "I've felt it, too."

Leon responded with a squeeze. "You understand I'm not asking you to marry me?" he asked, the fear of some form of feminine lassoing of a masculine wild animal apparent on his face.

"No?" Casey responded, her hand relinquishing his with just a barely perceptible shift in pressure.

"And I don't even think we should live together," Leon continued. His most basic insecurities fueled him to keep talking even as he had the barest of inklings that he should just shut up.

"Oh," she said, now placing her hand on her own lap.

"I'm just saying that you should move back to Alaska because it's better for you," Leon continued. "I want you to be happy, and I think we can, well, see each other."

"See each other?" Casey repeated coldly.

"You know I've always told you that I'm not one for marriage. In fact, I have always known that I'm not a marrying kind of guy. I've never told you any lies about that point."

"So let me get this straight," Casey said, standing up and pacing the room. "I'm supposed to give up my chance to work for one of the finest universities in the country and move back to Alaska, all so that I can 'see' you at your convenience?"

Her precise and angry tone had, at last, made him realize she didn't go along with his proposition.

"I'm telling you that I think there's something between us. There's something that makes me want you even when I think you're the most irritating woman ever placed on the face of the earth. There's something that makes me think that I never really wanted anyone else. There's something, in a world where getting along with your fellow human being is a rare and precious thing, that we should pay attention to."

"And I think," Casey said, her voice cold and prim, "that you have all the qualities I have never wanted in a man."

"That's not true! I'm steady when you're the kind of woman who needs a steady man. I'm wonderful with your baby when you need someone to be a father to Joseph. I'm passionate about you when you need passion to persuade you. Just because I don't have the externals—like a degree or a snobbish interest in opera..."

"Or a willingness to promise your love to me in a very simple civil or religious ceremony?" she supplied, a bemused expression coming over her face.

He was startled, and for a few moments waffled between blinding anger and laughter. She had stated the most simple truth between them; he knew now, with utter clarity, why their relationship could never work. She needed the powerful promises of marriage to give her the sense of security that she craved. She could forgive him the rest—the lack of education and the snobbishness she seemed to have—they were all smoke screens for the real needs she had.

And he knew he could not—not yet, anyway—give in to her.

A shriek from Joseph, along with an upturned bowl of strained peaches, was enough to break the emotion-packed moment. Casey and Leon were both glad to have an excuse to halt the conversation.

They ate dinner, hamburgers with juicy, voluptuous tomatoes. And the surprise of the evening was a deliciously spicy cornucopia of potatoes, green peppers and onions that Leon claimed was his own recipe. After dinner, it looked as though Joseph was sleepy, so Casey put the baby to bed, for once skipping their usual bedtime ritual of a bath.

When she returned to the kitchen, Leon had scooped ice cream into bowls for them. They ate on the back porch, exchanging stories about their childhoods, their lives in Alaska, even their dreams for the future, though they somehow knew not to speak too much about a future that they both knew would not include the other.

At some point, they fell silent, watching the late-summer fireflies blink in the dark night. Casey drained her glass of diet soda and leaned back in her chair, letting herself relax.

Leon put his hand on hers, and though she felt a shiver of frightening passion at his touch, she also realized that his touch presaged some wordless request for her trust.

"I will miss you," he said quietly.

"I will miss you," she responded, for one desperate moment wishing she could choose to return to Alaska with him. But that would be impossible.

She didn't know that Leon would, by morning, have one last desperate trick up his sleeve.

Casey awoke early, before the dawn came. She went to the backyard and stood in her bathrobe, sipping a cup of coffee she had hastily made. All the nervousness she had so carefully suppressed came to the surface. She was terrified. Of speaking in public, of meeting new people, of having to represent the man she had been married to. Oh, Robert, she thought, I sure hope I do you proud.

And suddenly, the sun suffused the backyard with light, silhouetting the leaves of the trees overhead. She felt a calm pass through her, and she was certain, for the first and last time of her life, that Robert was with her again. He seemed to put his arm around her, to comfort her, to reassure her that she was not going to let him down. And also, he released her, letting her move toward her future—

whether that future was in Chicago or in Alaska, whether with Leon or on her own.

She removed her wedding and engagement rings from her right hand. Maybe it was time to put them away, to keep them for Joseph to give to the woman he loved when he grew up. Robert would be happy to have her move on. He had loved her, and understood the love that she had given him in return...because even if it was limited, it was still love.

Grateful, she let the feeling remain with her, unwilling to move on, unwilling to let the specialness of that moment go. But in another few minutes, she heard the distant, though familiar, cry of her baby, and she went back into the house.

"Casey, would you get away from those curtains!" Harry yelled. He was surrounded by five student aides, each clamoring for his attention to some last-minute detail regarding the lecture, the exhibit, the afternoon's reception.

Casey pulled back from the stage curtain, where she had been sneaking peeks out at the audience for the past few minutes. Her stomach was churning. There had to be at least four hundred people crowded in the auditorium. And they had all come to see her.

It was enough to make her run screaming.

Two assistants of Harry's, both serious-looking young men with khaki pants and white shirts, were arguing about the placement of a panel of grass baskets. Harry cut short their comments and made a quick decision. And then all four of his assistants melted away, off to find another emergency.

Harry came up behind her.

"Come on, Casey, why don't you sit down back here," he said, leading her to a chair behind the curtain rope. "Just stay out of the way."

Casey sat down, her hands gripped around her lecture notes, already soaked with sweat.

"How long is it before I go on?" Casey asked, the lump in her throat making it difficult to talk. If it was this bad now, what was it going to be like when she had to face the audience?

"Just ten minutes," Harry answered.

The flurry of activity around them swelled; people ran back and forth, setting up the screen for the slides she would present as part of her lecture, testing the lighting and the sound equipment.

"Harry! Harry!" someone called. "We've got a problem with the kleig lights!"

"I've got to go," Harry explained to Casey. "Just promise to stay right here. Don't think that if you can observe the audience, they can't observe you. They'll think you're a silly little schoolgirl, instead of an important anthropological researcher."

He left Casey standing with her mouth still wide open in surprise. Important anthropological researcher? No one could possibly believe that.

Or could they?

"Having fun?" Leon asked, startling her with how quietly he had come up to her.

"Oh, I'm sorry, I didn't see you."

He looked wonderful in his suit. He looked as if he belonged in that sophisticated academic setting, every bit as much as any of the stuffed shirts in the audience. Except he was so much more handsome, with a virility that couldn't be hidden by silk ties or by cotton button-downs.

There was something odd about his tone, something a little too blasé considering their conversation of the night before. He had seemed perfectly relaxed this entire day, at ease in a way that didn't gel with the words they had flung at each other the night before.

Yes, something was different about Leon—and it wasn't just the new clothes.

"You don't need to be scared," he said soothingly. "Joseph's fine. Ginger will take good care of him until you return."

Ginger was the daughter of the controller at Meig's Airfield. Of course, her father was good friends with Leon. And of course, Ginger had been only too happy to help out a friend of the family. Ginger had arrived at ten in the morning, had played with Joseph for an hour before Casey even left. By the time Casey walked out the door, Joseph felt as though it was a holiday—getting to stay with an old friend.

"I'm not scared about the baby-sitter," Casey said. "It's this speech. It's making me shake and my throat is all dry."

"Maybe you should get a glass of water," Leon suggested, bending forward and nearly colliding with her head. "Sorry," he explained. "That guy almost hit me with the slide projector."

Casey stared at the projector as it was put into place at the center of the stage.

"I can't leave my seat," she explained. "Harry was quite adamant about that."

"How about if I get you a glass of water then?"

"Think you can negotiate between all those people?" she asked, gesturing at the rush of workmen and technicians.

"Somehow I think for a simple glass of water, I'll manage."

And he disappeared into the folds of the backstage curtains. Casey looked around, locating Harry amidst a crowd of noisy assistants, and waited for him to return to her.

"You have about two minutes before we start," he said. "The dean is going to announce you. She's already onstage, in front of the curtain."

She heard the beginnings of an introduction. From behind the thick curtains separating her from the audience, it was difficult to pick up everything. She caught snatches of it, though, and it embarrassed her: brilliant, thoughtful, important, ground-breaking work on a vanishing culture.

She was supposed to walk toward the lectern, face the crowd, look out into a sea of faces, brave the interrogation-style barrage of lights.

The applause died, and the dean, a smartly dressed, middle-aged woman, was signaling Casey to come forward.

Casey squared her shoulders and tried her never-fail trick of hiding her emotions when she was particularly scared or nervous. Once again, as she had done in the plane with Leon, she pretended she was someone else, someone sophisticated and cosmopolitan, used to giving speeches like this all the time, someone—what were the dean's words?—brilliant and capable of ground-breaking research.

In a split second, she became that person and walked out into the middle of the stage. She placed her notes on the lectern. The dean smiled encouragingly at her, and exited the stage to stand next to Harry, who smiled broadly at her and gave her the thumbs-up signal.

I've got to do this one last thing for Robert, she thought, then I can figure out what's wrong with Leon, why he's acting so strangely this morning.

Putting aside her emotions, she adjusted the microphone and began her lecture. Within seconds, she was unaware of the two men backstage. She was unaware, even, of the audience. The only things that existed for her were the slides she had to present and the wonderful story of the Athabascan Indians—a story that others were bound to find interesting if only because of the extraordinary passion she had for her field.

At the end of the lecture, she allowed for questions. She was pleased by the level of interest the subject generated. After twenty minutes of responding to the insightful questions and observations, she noticed a man at the back of the auditorium. She couldn't see anything more than a shadow of his hand raised because the lights onstage were so bright.

"Yes, the man in back," she acknowledged him. And, when his voice didn't carry over the standing-room-only crowd, she added, "Please step forward and speak a little louder. I'm afraid I couldn't hear your question."

The blood rushed from her head as Leon strode briskly to the center of the auditorium.

"Yes, Ms. Stevens," he said loudly, his authoritative voice capturing the attention of the restless crowd. "I have just a few questions for you."

Chapter Eleven

Leon stepped up to the microphone, which had been placed at the center of the auditorium between two sections of seats. He nervously straightened his tie—a rope of silk that felt about as comfortable and as friendly as a noose. Four hundred audience members turned and shifted to get a better look at him. This impulse to ask his questions in broad daylight, in an auditorium packed with onlookers—an impulse that had overwhelmed him in its urgency—now seemed utterly insane. When he had asked Harry as they watched the Bears play the Packers the night before, poor innocent Harry had thought Leon's questions about Athabascan Indians and the courtship rituals of primitive cultures were simply curiosity. He had even put his arm around Leon, and had said something about how he had learned so much from Leon about football, poker and beer that he was happy to return the friendly favor by teaching Leon something.

Getting up and asking Casey some questions had seemed like such a good idea. Now it seemed the height of insanity.

But he had the attention of four hundred listeners, and he had to continue.

"And what is your question?" Casey prompted, and he knew—even from the hundred feet that separated them, from the icy tone of her voice and rigid set to her mouth—that she was furious.

Suddenly all the anthropology buzzwords that Harry had coached him with had dissolved in his head. Was he going to have to come off sounding like a hick in order to get his point across?

"Ms. Stevens, your research seems to have been rather scant when it comes to courtship and marriage rituals within the culture."

"And?"

He wanted to stop the charade and simply say, *For God's sakes, Casey, come back to Alaska.* But since the direct approach had already failed, he squared his shoulders and spoke into the microphone.

"My question is just what kind of courtship and marriage rituals does Athabascan culture promote?"

She seemed taken aback by the question. She had clearly been expecting something horrible from him, something antagonistic or embarrassing, something not nearly as subtle as what he had in mind.

"Their courtship rituals are the same as nearly the world over," she began slowly as she gathered her thoughts. "Men are primarily the initiators of courtship activity."

"And marriage?" Leon asked. "Isn't marriage generally initiated by women?"

"Well, it is true that a man may receive some 'encouragement' from the matriarch of the family or the village when he shows a great deal of interest in a single woman. Often the woman in question will engineer a meeting between the suitor and the matriarch in order to promote a marriage.''

"How soon does this encouragement begin?"

"Basically, as soon as the man shows any sign of interest.''

"Just like our culture," Leon mused. The audience laughed. Leon paused, and when the laughter died down, continued his questioning. "And why is it that women are concerned about him showing interest in a woman? Why do they steer the relationship toward marriage?''

"Because, as in other primitive cultures, a woman's future, her very life, is dependent on coming under a husband's protection," Casey explained, her voice irritable. "She needs his financial support, and if it is generally known that a male initiated serious courtship without a marriage proposal, she may be perceived as damaged or lacking in some way.''

Leon warmed to his subject, now confident that he could make his point.

"That sounds a little cold-blooded if you ask me," he said jauntily. "Makes a man feel a little funny, I would bet, if he knows that before she's willing to spend any time with him, he's got to come up with a lifetime commitment of support.''

She recognized the comment he was making about their own relationship and about his own feelings about marriage.

"Mr. Brodie, the men must get something out of it— there aren't any bachelors in any of the villages I have ever observed," she said primly.

They glared at each other, oblivious to the mirth of the audience. He started to turn away, defeated—knowing that his attempt to show her his objection to marriage had failed.

But Casey was now on the offensive, and in her blind attempt to strike back at what she saw as his efforts to embarrass her at what should have been her most shining moment, she didn't care if she hurt him.

"One more thing, Mr. Brodie, about marriage and courtship," she said. "It may seem cold-blooded to you, but the men who are most prized within the villages are the ones most able to provide their future brides with some sense of security. Thus, the most intelligent, financially successful males are the ones most sought after for marriage. Women, on the other hand, are trading their youth, beauty, and childbearing abilities and are sought after in proportion to those qualities. After all, it's a primitive culture," she continued, disregarding the dean, who had come out onto the stage. "And while in modern America, it is hoped that people come into marriage because of love and not because of some sort of quid pro quo, it is exactly what many people engage in today."

Leon leaned into the microphone's range.

"My point exactly, Ms. Stevens," he said.

She wanted the last word, she wanted the final say, but the dean, with a commanding wave of her hand, captured both the lectern and the audience's attention. While Casey stared at the audience, squinting her eyes to bring Leon Brodie into focus, she was only dimly aware of the praise being heaped upon her by the dean and the audience. As the last strains of the applause died out, she was led off the stage by the dean and put into Harry's hands.

"You were wonderful," he gushed, and he pulled her through a crush of people—all congratulations and handshakes. They quickly turned into an empty hallway, Harry determined to give Casey a few minutes to catch her breath before the cocktail reception began.

Casey leaned back against the wall and let the pent-up anxiety of the past months run into her jellylike legs.

"You made me think we need to talk to the university about sending you back out there for more fieldwork," Harry said, excitedly pacing. "You presented so many more intriguing questions. And your research methods are so exciting and so intimate with the culture. Casey, have you ever thought of putting together a book—a popular one, with photos and very little text . . . ?"

"May I offer my congratulations as well, Ms. Stevens?" Leon stood beside her, holding out his hand.

She glared at him, furious at the innocent look on his face. "You tried to ruin my lecture," she accused, ignoring his hand.

"Maybe I had better leave you two alone," Harry offered.

"No, Harry, don't leave me."

"Harry, don't go, I was just saying goodbye anyway," Leon said.

Harry shook his head. "I never get involved in these sorts of romantic problems," he explained. "I'm going to go check on the champagne. Casey, you need to be in the reception room soon to press the flesh and have your picture taken. Remember, every minute you spend in there is another dollar in alumni contributions."

He disappeared into the crowded auditorium.

Leon and Casey stared at each other for a few silent moments.

"I guess this is goodbye," Leon said.

"Why did you try to humiliate me up there?" Casey asked.

"I wasn't doing it to be mean," he answered quietly. "I was trying to get through to you. In a few minutes, you're going to walk into that crowded reception and you're going to forget about me. Everything we've ever felt for each other, and everything we ever could feel about each other will be gone. It'll disappear like so much melted snow."

"So?"

"So, I felt something for you, and I know you felt something for me. Something that started the moment your son was born, something much more powerful than either of us by ourselves. We're two very flawed human beings. I'm too arrogant and I've spent too much time alone. You're too scared to take chances on things and you think that no one's ever been as lonely as you. We're both flawed and yet, together, we could be better, we could be happy, we could be different."

"And now?" Casey asked, tears forming at the brims of her eyes.

"You won't budge an inch unless it all comes with guarantees. You want a marriage proposal before you even go on a first date, and you want a laundry list of credentials because you don't want to take it on faith that I'm smart or I'm steady or I'm not going to hurt you."

"And you?" she asked breathlessly, knowing that everything he had said was true, and everything he was about to say as well.

"I'm scared to marry, to commit, to tie myself down— I think it would mean somehow I'd been conquered. I can look at myself and say that's a flaw and yet I can't change it for you. I can't just announce that I'm going to marry you if you only agree to move back to Alaska and you'd never want me here in Chicago. I'm too much of a flyboy to give up the freedom that comes with an open sky."

Her tears fell and he kissed each one from her cheeks.

"Go on in there," he said, gesturing toward the reception room. "You've worked for it, you've sacrificed for it, you've dreamed about it."

"I won't see you again?"

He shook his head and pulled off his tie.

"Here, I'm never going to need this noose again," he said, pressing it into her hands. "I'm going back to Harry's and pick up my gear. I'll be out of Chicago within the hour."

She twisted the soft silk tie around her hands.

"I think I love you," she offered tentatively.

"You might," he answered, pulling her into his arms for a final embrace. "And I might love you. But I'm beginning to think that love is about being transformed. If we truly loved each other, we would become different people—every molecule, every cell, every inch of our bodies would change. We would take chances on our love, we would be bold with our words, and we would give up everything without a peep of complaint."

"Ms. Stevens, Ms. Stevens," one of Harry's many assistants, an earnest, serious-looking woman, interrupted them. "Ms. Stevens, you really do need to come to the reception."

Leon and Casey pulled apart, and Casey wiped away the tears on her face. She stared up into his gray-green eyes, barely aware of the assistant pulling at her sleeve.

"So long, flyboy," she whispered.

He nodded silently in reply and she let herself be led down the hallway toward the reception room. As she self-consciously shoved Leon's tie into her suit-coat pocket, she turned to see if he was still there, standing in the hallway. He was and, with a final salute, he disappeared down the staircase.

"Ms. Stevens," the assistant said, "I just wanted to tell you that I really enjoyed your lecture. My faculty adviser was telling me that Harvard was already interested in you...."

Whatever else the assistant had to say, it was lost as Casey entered the brightly lit reception hall; she was immediately swept into a whirlwind of handshaking and introductions, professors from competing universities and alumni from her own school, questions and congratulations. Someone handed her a small glass of champagne, and with only a moment allowed for mourning her loss, she joined in a toast to her success.

The rest of the week in Chicago was rushed—a second lecture at the exclusive University Club of Chicago, three—or was it four?—cocktail parties in her honor, interviews with several newspapers, an appearance on two Chicago talk shows. The blur of activity left her drained at the end of each day.

She collapsed each night in her bed at Harry's house, exhausted and drained. She didn't have a chance to return the phone calls from Harvard, from Yale, from Princeton. Without a doubt, she had become "hot" and, as Harry never failed in delighting to remind her, every university in the country was going to be courting her while she spent the visiting semester at the University of Chicago. Hopefully, he added, she would choose to stay.

Harry was kind and considerate, escorting her to each public appearance. Gently and graciously, he guided her, briefing her in the car beforehand about a particular journalist's slant, waiting with a cool glass of water after each grueling speech, introducing her to everyone, and then whisking her away for the next event.

She was doubly grateful that he found someone to care for Joseph on such short notice after Leon left. Sabrina was a graduate student, with fiery red hair and Irish good humor, with an obvious crush on Harry. She was good with Joseph, played with him for hours—peekaboo and patty cake. She didn't seem to mind the morning to midnight hours punctuated only by the between-events visits Casey squeezed out of her days.

Joseph was steadily working on destroying Harry's house, and try as Sabrina might to keep up with him, he had already toppled several expensive vases and had thrown up on a handmade Persian rug. It was hard for Casey not to notice that while Harry had an irritable look on his face when he discovered these accidents, his expression quickly changed to one of understanding when Sabrina was doing the explaining.

At the end of the week, they returned to the house after a final interview for a Sunday supplement. Casey gratefully sank into a heavy leather chair and kicked off her still-unfamiliar black pumps.

"I'm so tired I could sleep for a week," she sighed. "One thing I'll say for this city—it's so fast-paced. And the crowds! I don't know how you do it, Harry."

Harry came from the kitchen bearing a tray of sandwiches, a bottle of champagne and Baccarat glasses. He pushed a coffee table nearer to her chair and put the tray down.

"Simple, my dear," he said, sitting on a stool near her feet. "City living takes a certain stamina. Crowds, crime, noise, traffic, it's all easy to deal with after a while. Here, let's have a drink to celebrate—I do believe your visit has done wonders for me. I don't mean to be crass, my darling, but you've managed to persuade Mrs. Paley to put a few extra hundred thousand in the endowment kitty, so I believe we should raise our glasses to Mrs. Paley.''

"To Mrs. Paley," Casey agreed.

They drank together, Casey allowing herself a small, careful sip.

"And to Sabrina," she said. "She's been wonderful to me and Joseph. And you know, Harry, she really is very attractive.''

"You really think so? I was noticing, by the way, that she is quite beautiful. She has the most extraordinary eyes, and her hair is . . ." He looked at her thoughtfully. "She's not really my type, though, is she?''

"Haven't you decided to abandon having a type?"

"Well, I mean, you couldn't be suggesting . . ." Harry stared at her, a look of confusion and bafflement. "Sabrina?" he asked, finally.

Casey nodded.

Harry relaxed in his chair, leaning back into the cushions while he considered the idea. At last, he smiled.

"Sabrina," he repeated and stared off into space. Casey didn't notice when he appeared to reach some decision and to have dismissed the topic with a satisfied and bemused shake of his head.

"You're thinking of your flyboy again, aren't you?"

"How did you know?"

"Lucky guess. I found him a rather enjoyable young man—taught me football and a charming little venture called poker. He was nice enough to give me back his winnings his last evening.''

"I'm having a little trouble getting him out of my mind. Funny how everything's going exactly as I would want it— and yet . . ."

There was silence between them, punctuated only by the ticking of Harry's antique German grandfather clock.

"Lighten up," Harry commanded, jumping up and putting a record on the turntable. A bright, cheerful Mozart minuet wafted through the room. "Let's think about your future—after all, you're going to be visiting a few universities this fall as you make up your mind where you want to stay."

Later, Sabrina brought Joseph home. She invited the three of them—Joseph, Harry and Casey—to her mom's for dinner. Casey declined, saying she wanted some quiet time at home with Joseph. She hadn't had much time alone with him and, to be honest, she hadn't had much time alone with herself.

After she had played with Joseph and his activity center—a rectangular panel of knobs and buttons and bells—she let him sit on a central rug as she wandered around the guest room as restless as a cat. There were a hundred things she knew she should do, now that the hectic pace of the trip had been slowed. There was hand washing the pile of stockings, or writing a long, newsy letter to Skip—after a week of fitful postcards, he deserved more—or reading through the stack of newspapers she had been saving for when she had just the time she had now.

But she couldn't settle down, and then her gaze fell upon the tie, Leon's tie, carefully folded on the dressing table. She touched it, gaining comfort from the soft fabric, marveling at the color, so much like how she remembered the color of his eyes. Was it only this morning that she had woken to find her hands around the tie as if it were a teddy bear?

"This is what I've wanted, isn't it?" she asked aloud. "It is what I've always wanted."

But if it was, why was she so unhappy?

Chapter Twelve

"Are you going to sit there all morning daydreaming or what?"

Casey looked down at the kitchen table in front of her. It held a coffee cup, a letter from Harry announcing his engagement to Sabrina, and the pile of paperwork that the university required as a condition of its research grant.

It was two weeks since she had returned to Alaska.

As long as she lived, she'd never forget Skip's face when he had gruffly answered the door.

"Frango mints?" she had asked innocently, holding out to him the candies from Marshall Field's in Chicago that he loved so much.

Now, Skip stood by the kitchen counter, waiting for an answer.

"Sorry," Casey said. "What were you saying?"

He threw up his hands in a gesture of mock despair.

"I thought you'd be happy, now that you're back, settled in, working on this new project," Skip said. "But every once in a while, you start this staring off into space business.''

He poured himself a cup of coffee, and nimbly stepping over Joseph's blocks, sat down across from her.

"Dammit, Casey, I'm worried about you. I'm happy you came back, but something's been troubling you. What is it?''

Casey turned around to the makeshift playpen she had constructed for her son out of blankets and pillows. Joseph was happily stacking blocks and bright plastic rings. He looked up at Skip and Casey and smiled.

"Gabadaba," he said, and gestured at his toys.

"Someday he's going to actually make sense," Skip said, sipping his coffee with a faraway look in his eyes. "I can't wait for that day."

"I'm not sure how to explain it, Skip, but didn't you tell me once about how it would be nice for Joseph to have a father, for me to have a husband?''

"Yeah, and you've decided you want one—a man?''

She shrugged, embarrassed by his straightforward answer, knowing that he was thinking of the one man who had haunted her dreams and her thoughts for months.

Leon.

Why, oh why couldn't she forget him? He certainly had forgotten her by now. Why couldn't she get him out of her head?

It was simple. She was in love.

When she woke last night from a dream of passion, it was Leon—strong and virile—she was dreaming of. Casey blushed involuntarily, thinking of the dream that had caused her to startle awake in a hot, steamy sweat.

Skip stood up and put his coffee cup in the sink.

"I'm going in for supplies later this morning. After I do inventory, that is. You want to join me?''

Casey put her papers in a neat stack and snapped the cap on her pen.

"I'd love to," she said.

He picked up Joseph and, with Casey following, took him out to the bar area.

Inventory took all morning, a nearly mindless task of checking all the supplies: beer, kerosene, food. Casey and Joseph followed Skip through the bar, the upstairs, the kitchen, counting jars and bottles, cans and cartons. At the end of the morning, they had a sizable list of the supplies they needed.

A contingent of trappers—five parka-clad, stubbly-cheeked men—came in for beers and some lunch. Casey helped Skip put the burgers on the grill, and served the men their beers. As the men drank, they became more exuberant, loudly swapping hunting stories from winters past.

Casey sat at the fireplace, idly listening to the men talk. Every once in a while, she offered her opinion—on the hunting that year, the salmon catch, whether the winter was as tough as last year. The men listened to her with the interest and respect one must give to a true Alaskan. She had proved herself, after all, and she was no mere newcomer to the frozen country.

A few more customers arrived: a man and wife from Fort Yukon on their way back to their own cabin, a group of tourists from the lower forty-eight. Skip's Place was busy for several hours; before Casey knew it, it was seven o'clock, and Joseph was yawning and anxious for bed— even if he didn't know it himself.

"I wish we would have gotten into Fort Yukon today," Skip confided in her as she helped make up the bed in one of the four guest rooms. The tour group had decided to stay the night. "There's supposed to be a storm coming in tomorrow, and these guys have run me clear out of beer."

"Why don't I go tomorrow with Joseph?" Casey suggested, smoothing down the worn sheet. The guest rooms were never very elegant, but they were clean and warm, two very important things at the top of the world.

"Deal."

"Let me put Joseph to bed now, and I'll come down and help with the cleanup."

Casey went into Joseph's room and picked him up from the playpen. She put him on the changing table and began the daunting task of changing the diaper of the squirming, twisting, wriggling baby boy. Ordinarily she played with Joseph, but tonight she felt distracted, her mind elsewhere. She noiselessly turned Joseph in the right direction and pulled on a fresh diaper.

It was Leon she kept thinking of, dammit. Leon as he had first entered the cabin—and the look of awe on his face when he had first held Joseph. Leon trying to feed Joseph. Leon at the Indian camp, gathering exhibit materials with her. Leon in her bedroom. Leon's kisses, his touch, her own passionate response...

"Come on, Mr. Joseph," she whispered, picking up the bottle of milk she had brought up, and taking Joseph to the rocking chair. "Time for your evening snack."

She sat in the softly lit room, listening to the bustle of guests finding their rooms. She was glad she had come home to Alaska, especially on a night like this—with the quiet camaraderie of Alaskan "insiders." At last the hotel was silent, and the only noise she heard was the gentle sucking and sighs of Joseph—contented to be doing the thing he liked best, in the place he liked most.

Everything she had liked best had been in Chicago. Everything she had ever dreamed of had been there. The university atmosphere of stimulating conversation and the intelligence of the students and faculty.

Harry had found her a wonderful full-time nanny, a woman that Joseph loved to distraction. The interviews with other universities convinced her that she was—and this shocked her—considered to be one of the leading anthropologists working directly in the field. The University of Chicago had quickly made her a permanent offer, not even waiting until the end of her "trial" semester. Even her social life had been everything she could have wanted; Harry quickly introduced her to a circle of friends who accepted her easily, and there was even a law professor, a single father of two, who was interested in seeing a little more of her than simply at the round of parties and outings that Harry organized.

It was everything she had ever wanted, and yet, it was nothing that she wanted. Every new cause for celebration—a favorable article about her work in yet another journal, an academic courtship initiated by another university, a newfound friend—left her increasingly numb. She couldn't rouse any enthusiasm, and found herself often lonely at night, mindlessly staring at the soft silk tie that Leon had left, that she had placed, with seeming casualness, on her dressing table.

When her honorarium from the university arrived, Casey had spent a weekend composing a note to enclose with her check to Leon. An entire box of filmy, linen stationery had been written on and then crumpled and discarded. At last, she had simply shoved a check for Leon into an envelope she borrowed from Harry and mailed it for the flyboy's services to Calvin Dodge—knowing that somehow, wherever that he was, Calvin would track his friend down.

How much she had wanted to write something bright and cheerful and witty. Something that would have told Leon how wonderful her new life was. How successful she was. How happy she was.

But all she had left was sadness, an aching in her throat that made her tremble at the thought of Alaska, of Skip's hotel at the top of the world, of Leon.

When she applied for a grant to continue her work—now it no longer seemed just Robert's work—the university was happy to provide funding and Harry's only condition was that she come back to Chicago twice a year for a round of lectures and talks.

She told everyone it was because she missed the wide open spaces of Alaska, that she missed the solitude of a winter night, that she missed Skip and the hotel's guests, that she missed the villages and the Athabascan villagers that she had developed relationships with in the past years.

She said all this, and yet she knew it wasn't quite true.

She missed Leon and though she wasn't prepared to change the way she felt about marriage—about the importance of creating a relationship that was one man, one woman—she knew she had changed her feelings about Leon. She had changed, and hadn't Leon said that love was about change? She had changed into someone confident enough about her choices to know that Chicago and the rarified atmosphere of the campus community wasn't for her. She had changed into someone who knew exactly the man for her, not merely a man who had the credentials she thought others deemed important.

But if love had changed her, had it changed Leon?

And if it hadn't?

If he was unable to come to her, there was nothing more that could be done.

Belinda Dodge settled her large frame—she had once laughingly told Leon that she preferred to be thought of as voluptuous—onto the counter stool. Leon could see out of the corner of his eye that her lips were pursed in a manner that suggested a lecture was coming. A lecture about his social life.

He decided to ignore her for as long as he could, so he returned his attention to his cards.

"Eights?" David Dodge asked, peering over his own hand. Though only five, he concentrated on his game like a regular card shark. Like father, like son, Leon thought, remembering the many poker games he had lost to David's father, Calvin.

"Go fish," Leon replied.

The Dodge kitchen was a brightly lit one, with bubble-gum-pink curtains, sunshine-colored appliances and an assortment of children's toys strewn around the floor. Belinda Dodge wasn't a great housekeeper, and she made few apologies about that.

But the Dodge house resonated with human warmth, a quality that Leon had found keeping him longer than the weekend he had told them he would be staying. What had it been, two months? Two months since he had returned from Chicago.

Two months since he had seen Casey.

Belinda wasn't put off by Leon ignoring her. In fact, it seemed to galvanize her to action. She took a long drink of her soda and put her glass on the table with a loud clank designed to catch the attention of the two males at the table. Instead both stared at their cards, hypnotized.

"Leon, I want to talk to you," Belinda said at last.

"Can't you see I'm busy?" Leon asked. "Fives."

David slapped down a card with an exaggerated air of disgust.

"Leon, I want to know why you have been moping around this house for weeks on end, and more to the point, I just found out you haven't called Diane. It's Friday night. A young man like you should be out on the town. Now, she's a nice girl and I told her I gave you her phone number."

Diane was the woman Belinda had set him up with most recently. First, there was Anne the dental technician. Then there were Barbara and Alice, both bartenders. Then Merrill the secretary. Or was she the beautician? They were all blondes. Belinda had taken seriously the joking demand that Leon had made that any woman she set him up with had to be a blonde—anything to contrast with and make him forget Casey's chestnut hair.

And now Diane, who owned a grocery store. But Leon didn't know whether she was a blonde, because he hadn't yet seen her. He hadn't even called her, although he still had the scrap of paper with her phone number that Belinda had given him. Somewhere.

"I'm just not interested," Leon said, studying his cards. "She might be a nice girl, friendly and everything. Just not my type. Nines."

David plunked down another two cards, which Leon quickly picked up.

"I don't think you have a type anymore," Belinda said. "It's damned unnatural to be spending every night at home like this. You haven't gone out with any of these women I've scared up for you. And available women in Alaska are pretty scarce. I'm tired of having to explain why you don't call after I sell you to these women. I think you don't want to go out with anyone."

"Bingo," Leon murmured quietly.

"Mom, can't you leave him alone?" David asked. "He's playing go-fish with me."

"Young man, I seem to recall your bedtime as having come up nearly a half hour ago," Belinda said. "I think you better mosey on up to bed. Why don't you go find Daddy and have him read you your Bible story?"

"Mom!" David screeched.

"No back talk," Belinda insisted. "Up to bed."

"Yeah, tough guy, up to bed," Leon added. "I'll tell you what, if you do what your mom asks, I'll come up and read you your Bible story."

"Will you tell me another one of your flying stories?" David pleaded.

"Sure thing."

David threw down his cards and got up from his chair. He gave his mom a quick kiss.

"Don't take too long, Leon!" he shouted as he left the kitchen.

Belinda leaned back and drank from her glass. Leon hummed a children's song while he gathered the cards, some ditty David had taught him that morning and he couldn't get out of his head.

"What I mean is, we're worried that you're not happy. You don't go out except when we—" she searched for the right word "—foist some woman on you on a thinly disguised double date. Sometimes I think you're still nursing a broken heart."

Leon felt the bitterness, the bitterness he had been feeling for months, rise into his throat. He couldn't forget her, he couldn't burn her out of his heart with whiskey, he couldn't replace her in his dreams with a voluptuous blonde. It killed his pride to admit it. And it wasn't something he could admit often—even to himself.

Leon abruptly threw the cards down on the table. "I don't want to talk about some broken heart."

"Leon, I'm your friend, or at least, I'd like to think I'm your friend. I know I've only known you for a short time."

Leon absentmindedly reclaimed the cards. Belinda's voice faltered and she fell silent. The kitchen clock hummed, and both could hear David upstairs talking to his stuffed animals, putting each of them to bed.

"I hear she's come back. She's back at Skip's Place."

Leon felt suspicion slice through him. "How do you know?"

"We have the produce run to Fort Yukon. I get a report from the pilot every week. He gets his weekly report from Skip, who is, by the way, damned and determined to get you two back together again. Last I hear, she's there—came back two weeks ago, and I heard about it this morning."

Casey. In Alaska. Within reach. He could picture the tousle of red-brown hair, eyes the color of fine blue ink, and her natural perfume. He leaned back in his chair and closed his eyes. Somehow she had always smelled of flowers, very delicate flowers. He opened his eyes and shook his head.

"What's the use? She probably doesn't want to have anything to do with me." Leon's thoughts briefly turned to when he had gotten her check, final payment for his services. He had looked for a note, some personal touch and the disappointment he had felt when there was none had stayed with him for days. Any note, even a falsely cheerful one, would have made him waver, made him think of giving up everything in his life—flying, freedom, Alaska—to go to Chicago.

"Leon, for someone so smart, you're awfully dumb about women sometimes." Belinda laughed. "What do you think she's doing back in Alaska?"

"Fieldwork," he muttered.

Leon let himself start to hope again. For the first time since he had returned to Alaska. Two months sure felt like a century for him to be away from Casey. The nights were the worst, when there wasn't anything to distract him from thinking about her. From dreaming.

"But why do I have to go chasing after her?" Leon felt a jolt of panic at the thought of meeting Casey again. Why is it something I want so much, he thought, and yet fear so much?

"Look, Calvin didn't want to marry me when he first met me," Belinda said, lowering her voice to a whisper. "I'm not a Playboy bunny type, in case you haven't noticed. So I asked him to marry me maybe seven times. Finally he said yes, but I'm sure glad I didn't give up after the first no. Or the sixth no, for that matter."

"Wait a minute. He told me he was the one doing the asking."

"Look, honey, if he wants to think he was the one doing the chasing, let him. As long as I got my man in the end." She leaned back with a satisfied grin on her face. At that moment, Leon had to admit Belinda was pretty—well, maybe even beautiful, suffused with the glow of love.

It was funny how a few months ago, he would have seen in that face a terrible feminine victory over masculine freedom. Now he saw something different, something extraordinary...

"Are you going to tell me a bedtime story, or what?"

The two adults turned around and in the doorway, David stood, holding his teddy bear and waiting for Leon.

"You brushed your teeth and washed your face?" Belinda asked.

"Yes, Mommy," David answered. "I'm all ready for bed."

He hurried forward and put his arms around Belinda, digging his head into her shoulder.

"I love you, honey," she said.

"I love you, too, Mommy."

Leon stood up, anxious not to let the tender good-nights make him long for something he might never have. Had he decided he wanted a different, more domestic life? Had he changed one evening when he had helped Belinda make dinner? Had he changed some morning when he sat with the entire Dodge family, eating pancakes and reading the newspapers? Had some transformation occurred one time when he was telling David a bedtime story, watching the look of adoration and respect the five-year-old gave him?

Or had it been earlier? When he took Joseph out on the town in Chicago, holding the little baby in his arms? When he fed him, helping Casey and Skip? Or even earlier—when he first saw her?

As frightening as it was, he believed he might be a different man than the one that had flown the skies a scant few months ago.

Of course I'm perfect for her, he thought, his confidence returning—a confidence shattered in Chicago. *I'm strong in ways that other men can't even imagine. I'm going to love her son in a way no other man can. But most of all, I'll love her,* Leon thought. *I know the real Casey,* Leon reminded himself, *the flesh and blood Casey. And I love that Casey.*

And besides, I need her, a small voice inside his head reminded him.

Somehow David fell asleep in the middle of his story, so Leon tucked the blankets around the boy and turned off the lights and walked out into the hallway. Calvin stood in the doorway to the master bedroom.

"Calvin, I need one more favor."

"What's that?"

"I'm going to be out for a while, I've got some business to attend to."

Chapter Thirteen

The road didn't get any easier. The snow made the horizon come up closer and closer to the dashboard, making her headlights useless. The gravel road was sheeted with ice and the wheels balked at every turn, at every elevation.

Casey was thankful, and yet somehow worried, that Joseph, tired from the excitement of a shopping excursion to Fort Yukon, had closed his eyes and slept quietly in his car seat. Thankful because it was hard to concentrate on driving when he complained in his seat, as he usually did.

But worried because she was certain his sleepiness signaled sickness. He had been coughing, an itchy, persistent cough—the kind that made every mother cringe. And his forehead had seemed just a bit warm, not enough to panic and run to the doctor, but enough to make her just a little nervous.

And she was not happy with her own body. She, too,

wanted to sleep and had to fight with herself to keep awake. She felt strangely disoriented, probably from fever.

Her throat had become tight and constricted, and each breath felt as if it was forced through a straw.

She loosened her jacket collar and thought about turning down the heat. But Joseph would need the warmth. Even in his snowsuit, he needed the protection the blast of hot air from under the dashboard provided, so she put the heat back on.

Just let me get Joseph home safely, she prayed.

Home.

That's what she must think Skip's Place was. The warmth of that fireplace, the smell of Skip's strong coffee, the soft flannel sheets—that was her home, the place where she felt all the safety and love that the word home encompassed.

At last, after a tortured hour of driving, the familiar landmarks reassured her. She passed trees and bushes that she didn't even know she would recognize. She pressed the accelerator and drove the Land Rover up the last hill before Skip's Place came into view.

"Thank God," she whispered, applying the remaining strength she had to maneuvering the Land Rover next to the cabin. She pressed vehemently on the horn, startling Joseph awake. But she needed Skip's help. Desperately.

The cabin door opened, bringing a shivering, flannel-robed Skip out to meet her.

"Get Joseph!" she shouted, trying to make her hoarse voice heard above the whistling wind.

Skip ran around to the passenger door and pulled Joseph into his arms. The three hurried into the cabin, slamming the door behind them.

"You look like hell," Skip said, with his usual tact. "You all right?"

"No," said Casey, shaking her head. "I'm not doing too well. Joseph isn't doing too well, either. Can you get off Joseph's snowsuit? I'm going to sit down. Just for a minute."

Skip unzipped Joseph's suit.

"You could fry an egg on this baby's skin!" he exclaimed. And Joseph, normally so happy at seeing his old and trusted friend, merely reached out his arms to his mother.

Casey sat him on her lap and put her arms around him. *God, don't let me lose him,* she prayed.

Leon pounded at the door. Damn! he thought, it's cold as…well, it was cold. He rubbed his leather-gloved hands together and waited for a response. The whistling wind made it impossible to hear whether there was anyone in the cabin. He raised his fist at the door again.

Then it was flung open.

Skip stood in the doorway, a red-faced howling Joseph in his arms.

"Get in here, you have the most annoying habit of always letting the heat out, flyboy," Skip said, backing away from the door to let Leon in. He expressed no surprise at seeing Leon, or even acknowledged that it had been nearly three months since they had last seen each other.

Leon kicked at the door frame with his boots, letting a clump of snow fall to the ground. He closed the door behind him, letting the warmth of the roaring fire chase away his cold.

"Skip, what's going on?" he asked, barely able to get his voice high enough to drown out Joseph's crying. The baby had tears running down his eyes, his cheeks were a brilliant red, and he struggled wildly against Skip's arms.

"Casey's sick, Joseph's sick, and I can't do everything around here," Skip said, leading Leon into the kitchen. "What took you so long?"

"What do you mean?"

Skip brought Joseph to his high chair. The baby arched his back, refusing to sit down. Skip gave up and put Joseph over his shoulder, swaying to and fro. Joseph's cries were reduced to soft, pitiful moans.

"What I meant was, why did you wait so long?" Skip asked. "You waited until she's damned near dead."

"What?"

"She's upstairs—got a fever over a hundred and two. I can't let Joseph near her 'cause he's just starting to feel better. The crying's a good sign. Don't worry, he's just grouchy now. Wouldn't you be? I can't do everything here. You want to take care of her or the baby?"

"I'll take her, thanks," Leon said, heading out of the kitchen.

He raced to her room, taking the stairs two at a time. He found her on the bed, her pale legs had kicked the sheets and blankets away from her. Her breathing was restless, her skin fiery to the touch. Her lashes fluttered briefly as he stroked her cheek. She looked at him briefly, her face registering no look of recognition. And then she fell back into her troubled, feverish sleep.

He went to the adjacent bathroom and filled a pan with cool water. He searched the medicine cabinet for rubbing alcohol and found an extra set of sheets in the cabinet next to the sink. He threw a couple of towels over his shoulder and, loaded down, went back into the bedroom.

He had never really cared for anyone, never felt another person's needs as anything more than an annoyance. But as he tenderly bathed her flushed skin with a mixture of cool water and rubbing alcohol, he felt the warmth and satisfaction of being needed.

He lifted her up, smiling at her faint, sleep-clouded resistance, and changed the sheets. After making her comfortable, he sat in a chair next to her bed, watching over her while she struggled with her fever. He knew there wasn't much to do but wait.

He jumped up at the gentle knock on the door. As he reached the door, Skip came in with a sleeping Joseph slung over his shoulders.

"I got some food into him," Skip said. "He's a lot happier now. I got some soup downstairs for you."

Leon shook his head.

"I'm not very hungry. I'll stay up here," he said, sitting back into his chair.

"Suit yourself," Skip said with a shrug and left the room.

The night was long, weighted with worry for Leon. He bathed her several times, each time marveling at her beauty—the slender ankles, the delicate curve of her hips.

After a last alcohol bath, her fever broke and he mopped the sweat from her forehead. She drank water from the cup he held to her lips.

He refused Skip's offer of a meal, of a beer, of company, of relief.

Mostly, he waited. Waiting wasn't something Leon had ever spent a lot of time doing, certainly never for a woman. He was an active, restless man, used to getting what he wanted by expending some energy. Now he knew that the most important thing he could do was nothing—to just let nature take its course.

He knew that something inside of him had changed slowly, imperceptibly. Maybe the process had even begun when he was in Chicago, when he had held Casey in his arms even as he had told her that they couldn't be together. He had changed, and he hoped that she had changed, too, because it wouldn't work otherwise.

He wasn't sure when he fell asleep. It must have been after three o'clock, because that was the last time he remembered checking the clock. The cabin was already quiet, Skip and Joseph long gone to sleep, the howling storm quiet once again.

He didn't need to open his eyes to know where he was. It always amazed him how a few hours sleep spent curled even in a cockpit, the floor of an airport lobby or a restaurant booth, could make a man's bones ache. And the rocking chair next to Casey's bed was no exception. He stretched his legs and arms out and opened his eyes.

She was looking at him, her blue eyes strained, but steady.

"How long have you been awake?" he asked. His eyes followed her gaze at the clock. Ten o'clock in the morning.

"I think I woke up a half hour ago," she said. "I've been pretty sick?"

"Yeah, Skip says you've been out since Friday," Leon said, leaning forward and rubbing his ankles. *I must be getting old,* he thought, *all my joints ache.*

"What's today?"

"Monday."

"And my baby?"

"He's fine. If you're really quiet you can hear them downstairs playing."

"Why did you come back?"

She asked with such directness that he was momentarily put off his guard. He didn't know how to put his feelings into words; he had never tried before. He stood up.

"I was just passing through," he said, hoping she would catch the joking tone in his voice. "I'm going to run downstairs and get some soup for you. You have a lot of catching up to do in the drink-plenty-of-liquids, get-lots-of-rest department."

"Oh, I think I've gotten the rest," she said, and with the speed of a cat, flung off the sheets and sat up. But her hand went up to her forehead, and she fell back to her pillow. "I'm sorry, I didn't realize how woozy I'd feel."

"You'll be like that for a few days," Leon said. "But I don't think you have a fever anymore."

He put his hand out to her forehead, brushing his fingers lightly against her cheeks as he did so. Though he had seen and touched all of her in the past night, this contact seemed so much more intimate. Her eyes flew up, looking at him with a soft fear—and he wondered if she was as scared as he was of intimacy, of love.

"No, I don't think I have a fever anymore," she said quietly, as he drew his hand away.

"Well, then I'll just get you some soup," Leon said brusquely and headed for the door. Why couldn't he say what was on his mind? Just tell her he came back for her, because he wanted her, because he had been wrong to leave without a simple goodbye because he loved her?

Leon suddenly felt incompetent, somehow incapable of negotiating the simple communications that other people managed every day.

He trotted down the stairs and headed for the kitchen. At least getting some soup was something he could handle. As he flung open the door to the kitchen, he heard a loud *thwack!* He had run headlong into Skip.

"Don't you ever watch where you're going?" Skip asked, holding his nose. "I think you broke all the bones in my face."

"Sorry," Leon said, feeling even more incompetent. "I was just coming down for some soup for Casey. She's awake now. Fever's gone."

"Well, thank goodness. Grab a bowl and get on up there."

Skip settled into his chair at the table and pulled out the crossword puzzle from the *Anchorage Digest.*

Joseph sat on the floor, playing with blocks, putting them into a pan Skip had let him play with, and then taking them back out.

Leon made up a tray of soup and crackers and tea and headed for the kitchen door.

Casey hastily pulled the comb through her hair. The tube of mascara, long unused, was dry. But she had found a tube of lipstick, Rosy Night, in the nightstand. Casey looked into the pocket mirror she had also found.

The reflection, less a glamour girl than a pale, drawn woman, didn't satisfy her. Was it silly to want to look wonderful for him? To wish that she could transform herself into the kind of beauty she was certain he wanted?

She heard his rough, heavy footsteps on the stairs, and she quickly threw comb, lipstick and mirror back into the nightstand, shoving the drawer closed with a furtive glance at the door.

"You feel any better?" Leon asked, softly kicking the door closed behind him. He carried a tray of steaming, fragrant soup. Her salivary glands kicked into overdrive. It made her mouth hurt to be this hungry!

"Yeah, sure," she said. She looked up into his eyes, seeking the reassurance that only a lover can give. She leaned back, gratified. Something in him had changed. There was a tenderness there that she had never seen before. Maybe he wasn't the sort of man to settle down with one woman, but she was willing to take what he offered—whatever his terms—to have that tender look directed her way.

Leon placed the tray on the nightstand and motioned for her to move over on the bed. Casey complied, shifting her body to the center of the bed. Leon sat on the edge of the bed, and put the bowl on his lap.

"What are you going to do?" she asked.

"I'm going to feed you," he said in an authoritative tone that left no room for argument.

Casey leaned back and let him spoon the savory liquid into her mouth.

"Why are you taking such good care of me?" she asked. She closed her eyes, enjoying the way that the liquid seemed to warm her whole body.

He put his spoon back on the nightstand and looked at her, a flicker of harsh anger passing over his face.

"Look, I'm not very good at expressing my feelings," he said. "I always thought that the kind of people who say 'I love you' all the time are looking for some type of reassurance that is sort of shallow and easy to hand out. It doesn't mean nearly as much as actions."

She felt herself blush with embarrassment. She hadn't meant to put him on the spot—not after she had felt the emptiness of his absence. She didn't want to scare him away again.

Leon put the bowl on the nightstand and put his arms around her, pulling her up to him.

"I'm just saying I can't change everything for you," he said. "Casey, there's never been another woman since I've met you. And, frankly, I know there's never going to be another again."

"Really?"

"You've ruined me." He laughed, but then his voice dropped. "I can't look at anyone else without thinking of you."

"So, it's not other women . . ."

"No, that's not it at all. The things I can't change are all those things that I'm sure made Robert so important to you. Education, being interested in cultural things. I'm never going to be able to talk about theater and art. I'll try to listen. . . .''

"Leon, you don't need to be someone else," she said. "I just want to know what you're feeling about me, about us, about . . .''

"Does this tell you what I'm feeling?"

The taste of his kiss was so rich, so fulfilling that she felt her whole body give in to him. She shuddered and, as the kiss ended and his mouth relinquished hers, she let her head fall backward. It had never been a fluke, she thought. His kisses were real.

And so was her matching passion.

He dropped his head to her throat, brushing her skin with his velvety lips. She smiled, joyful at the newfound pleasures. He lifted his head.

"Was that a knock?" Leon asked, clearly irritated.

Casey lifted her head.

"I think so," she whispered.

The knocking started again.

"If someone doesn't tell me they're alive in there, I'm coming in," Skip shouted through the door. "Enough lounging around."

With a flurry of shouted just-a-minutes, Casey and Leon positioned themselves into poses of studied casualness.

Skip opened the door, smiling mischievously. He balanced Joseph, a tray of sandwiches and a newspaper.

"Darned thing missed you," Skip said. "Ever try explaining to a baby that his mother is otherwise disposed with her boyfriend?"

"You could have come in anytime," Casey said. "We were just talking."

"Just talking," Leon repeated.

Skip looked from one to the other—Leon carefully reading his newspaper as if every word were vitally important to him, Casey intently cradling her baby.

"You both are either lying or you're the most boring couple I've ever met."

"Well, I'd like to know when we'd get any privacy to do anything more," Leon said.

"When you're married!" Skip said, with a harrumph.

And he turned heel and went out the door. Casey and Leon waited until the footsteps died down before they burst into mutual laughter.

Casey suddenly stopped laughing when she saw how Leon looked at her, how he searched her face, how he stared.

"What's the matter?" she asked, with what she hoped was a lighthearted tone.

"Maybe he's right. Casey, will you marry me?"

Casey felt her breath free itself from her lungs.

"Is that a proposal or a hypothetical?" she whispered, smiling up at him as they both remembered her question as he stood on the stairs in Harry's house.

"It's a proposal—something I was sure I'd never do. I've spent the months apart from you turning into husband material. If you're willing . . ."

"If I'm willing? Leon, while I've been away, I've turned into someone who wants more than anything else to be your wife."

He laughed and fell into the bed with her and Joseph. Since Joseph sat at the foot of the bed, entranced by a rattle, they assumed it was safe and their lips, hungry for the confirmation of their promises, met. But before their kiss could unfold, like the beautiful flower it was, Joseph leaped between them, giggling and squirming.

"Aren't we ever going to have any time alone?" Leon laughed, gathering up Joseph into his arms and tickling him.

As Casey looked up at the two males, she was so happy and content that her heart felt as light as air. Nothing could mar her contentment, her feeling that her future was an exciting possibility before her, a possibility to be shared.

Epilogue

"Casey, Casey," Leon murmured sleepily, pulling his head out from under his pillow. "Casey, would you please settle down? There's a man here who would like to get some sleep."

"Leon, it's time," Casey replied.

Sighing, Leon reached up and turned on the nightstand light. He squinted at the clock.

"Are you sure? I mean, it's three o'clock in the morning."

"Do you think a baby's going to say 'gee, I shouldn't come out into the world now because my daddy wants to get a good night's sleep'?"

Leon shook his head. It was hard to argue with women's logic.

"Aren't you excited?" Casey asked with disarming enthusiasm.

"Of course, I'm excited. It's my first baby—unless you count Joseph." He leaned forward so that his face disappeared in the goose-feather pillow. "I just wanted some sleep tonight, that's all."

"I'm starting a contraction," Casey announced.

Leon bolted upright, his sleepiness evaporating. He stood up, marveling at a wife who could simultaneously breathe deeply through a contraction and admire her husband's body. For it was clear from the look she gave him that the adoration, which had characterized their first months of marriage, hadn't dissipated simply because Casey carried his baby.

His baby!

Leon grabbed a pair of jeans and tried to insert both legs at once.

"Calm down," Casey pleaded, her contraction gone, her face relaxed.

"How can I calm down? This is my baby we're talking about," Leon exclaimed. He zipped up his jeans and threw on a sweater. "Where are my shoes?"

"In the closet," Casey answered sweetly.

Pacing like a caged animal around the room, Leon pulled on socks, fretted over where his watch was, picked up his shoes and then abandoned them.

"Are you all right?" he asked, frantic. "And by the way, where are my keys?"

He was irritated by Casey's calm, contemplative smile. "Aren't you nervous?"

"We went through this with Joseph," she replied, shrugging her shoulders. She shifted her weight, sliding into a sitting position. Leon hadn't seen her sit up without help in months. "By the way, your keys are on the dresser."

While he wandered around, finding his keys, locating his wedding band, discovering the shoes he had earlier dropped, he was surprised that his wife was simply brushing her hair. When she pulled out a tube of lipstick and calmly applied some to her lips, he broke.

"Casey, how can you think about something like your appearance at a time like this?"

She looked puzzled.

"I only said it was time to go to the hospital, I didn't say it was a national emergency." Her tone was loving and gentle. He found himself in awe of her strength. "By the way, do you think I should wake up Joseph?"

"Casey, I thought we agreed we would let him sleep and I would try to fly back in at the earliest opportunity to get both him and Skip."

"All right," she said. "Maybe I'll just go in and give him a kiss."

After she left, he stealthily pulled a small velvet box from the chest of drawers. Opening the box, he was pleased with his choice—a ring with two stones—a ruby, the birthstone of their new baby and a diamond, Joseph's birthstone.

As he stared at the simple setting of the two-stone ring, he was again amazed at how quickly he had come to think of Joseph as his own son. He knew in the coming years it would be important for Joseph to learn about the man who had fathered him. But there was no denying the extraordinary love he had for the little baby. So much that when Leon had told the jeweler in Anchorage that he wanted a simple ring to commemorate this happy day, there had been no question but to include Joseph's birthstone.

He put the velvet box into his jeans pocket and ran downstairs to wake Skip. A forty-five-minute flight into Fort Yukon, and maybe he'd be a father by sunrise.

When they buckled themselves into the plane, waving a last goodbye to Skip, Leon first became aware that his wife was in some pain. A cheerful smile couldn't hide the sweat that had beaded on her forehead and had made her hair bunch into damp curls. Nor could it hide the feathery lines of concern around her eyes. As they cruised over the dark Alaskan ground, he squeezed her hand, instantly reminded of the first time they had flown together.

And instantly grateful, as he often was, for the twists and turns of fate that had brought them together. He had matured, he knew. He had found a peace in being a husband and father—and even son-in-law to Skip—that reminded him that his earlier obsession with flight had been a means for running away from people.

He still enjoyed flying, but now he could enjoy being on the ground as well.

Under the reflective glow of the instrument panel, he could see the tension wash over Casey's face.

"Another one?" he asked.

She nodded.

They flew in silence until, after a minute, the contraction subsided.

"I want to tell you that this time is different," she said. "When I had Joseph, I panicked, I was so afraid, I felt so alone. Now I feel braver, not as scared."

"Just because you're married to me?"

"Yes, it's true. I used to have a method of doing things even when I was afraid. I would pretend to be someone else, someone braver, more glamorous, more sophisticated. And that someone else would do whatever it was that I was too afraid to do."

"And now?"

"Now I don't have to pretend. You've made me so happy, and I've become so secure with myself, with you, that I don't have to be someone else."

He nodded, thinking he knew exactly what she meant.

* * *

At 6:30 a.m., Leon Brodie, Jr., eight pounds, eleven ounces, entered the world kicking and screaming, every bit as contentious as his mother and father.

* * * * *

COMING NEXT MONTH

#826 STING OF THE SCORPION—Ginna Gray
Written in the Stars!
Jake Taggert was a true Scorpio—intense in all his passions,
and when he saw a chance for vengeance—he took it. But
Susannah Dushay was nobody's victim and *Jake* was about
to be stung!

#827 LOVE SHY—Marcine Smith
Social worker Jill Fulbright knew all about the agony of shyness—
she hid her own by helping others. But eccentric inventor
Daniel Holiday's diffidence gave her confidence—even when it came
to love....

#828 SHERMAN'S SURRENDER—Pat Tracy
Big-city businessman Jared Sherman refused to succumb to
Green River's small-town charm—or its charming librarian—until
Amelia Greene unveiled her plan to force his surrender in the battle
of love!

#829 FOR BRIAN'S SAKE—Patti Standard
When teacher Bethany Shaw accepted a position as nanny to
Mitchell Hawthorne's son, she hadn't expected to fall for them both.
Soon, Beth wanted to give Mitch lessons in love—for *her* sake....

#830 GOLD DIGGER—Arlene James
Professor Meyer Randolph didn't want his father's money—he
wanted his nurse! Elaine Newcomb's bedside manner made his
temperature rise. *Was* she a gold digger...or just pure gold?

#831 LADY IN DISTRESS—Brittany Young
Lovely widow Shelby Chassen wasn't about to chance love again, but
Parker Kincaid wouldn't let her go. The powerful attorney melted her
icy defenses, saved her life...and stole her heart....

AVAILABLE THIS MONTH:

SILHOUETTE®
OFFICIAL SWEEPSTAKES
RULES

NO PURCHASE NECESSARY

1. To enter, complete an Official Entry Form or 3" × 5" index card by hand-printing, in plain block letters, your complete name, address, phone number and age, and mailing it to: Silhouette Fashion A Whole New You Sweepstakes, P.O. Box 9056, Buffalo, NY 14269-9056.

   No responsibility is assumed for lost, late or misdirected mail. Entries must be sent separately with first class postage affixed, and be received no later than December 31, 1991 for eligibility.

2. Winners will be selected by D.L. Blair, Inc., an independent judging organization whose decisions are final, in random drawings to be held on January 30, 1992 in Blair, NE at 10:00 a.m. from among all eligible entries received.

3. The prizes to be awarded and their approximate retail values are as follows: Grand Prize — A brand-new Ford Explorer 4×4 plus a trip for two (2) to Hawaii, including round-trip air transportation, six (6) nights hotel accommodation, a $1,400 meal/spending money stipend and $2,000 cash toward a new fashion wardrobe (approximate value: $28,000) or $15,000 cash; two (2) Second Prizes — A trip to Hawaii, including round-trip air transportation, six (6) nights hotel accommodation, a $1,400 meal/spending money stipend and $2,000 cash toward a new fashion wardrobe (approximate value: $11,000) or $5,000 cash; three (3) Third Prizes — $2,000 cash toward a new fashion wardrobe. All prizes are valued in U.S. currency. Travel award air transportation is from the commercial airport nearest winner's home. Travel is subject to space and accommodation availability, and must be completed by June 30, 1993. Sweepstakes offer is open to residents of the U.S. and Canada who are 21 years of age or older as of December 31, 1991, except residents of Puerto Rico, employees and immediate family members of Torstar Corp., its affiliates, subsidiaries, and all agencies, entities and persons connected with the use, marketing, or conduct of this sweepstakes. All federal, state, provincial, municipal and local laws apply. Offer void wherever prohibited by law. Taxes and/or duties, applicable registration and licensing fees, are the sole responsibility of the winners. Any litigation within the province of Quebec respecting the conduct and awarding of a prize may be submitted to the Régie des loteries et courses du Québec. All prizes will be awarded; winners will be notified by mail. No substitution of prizes is permitted.

4. Potential winners must sign and return any required Affidavit of Eligibility/Release of Liability within 30 days of notification. In the event of noncompliance within this time period, the prize may be awarded to an alternate winner. Any prize or prize notification returned as undeliverable may result in the awarding of that prize to an alternate winner. By acceptance of their prize, winners consent to use of their names, photographs or their likenesses for purposes of advertising, trade and promotion on behalf of Torstar Corp. without further compensation. Canadian winners must correctly answer a time-limited arithmetical question in order to be awarded a prize.

5. For a list of winners (available after 3/31/92), send a separate stamped, self-addressed envelope to: Silhouette Fashion A Whole New You Sweepstakes, P.O. Box 4665, Blair, NE 68009.

PREMIUM OFFER TERMS

To receive your gift, complete the Offer Certificate according to directions. Be certain to enclose the required number of "Fashion A Whole New You" proofs of product purchase (which are found on the last page of every specially marked "Fashion A Whole New You" Silhouette or Harlequin romance novel). Requests must be received no later than December 31, 1991. Limit: four (4) gifts per name, family, group, organization or address. Items depicted are for illustrative purposes only and may not be exactly as shown. Please allow 6 to 8 weeks for receipt of order. Offer good while quantities of gifts last. In the event an ordered gift is no longer available, you will receive a free, previously unpublished Silhouette or Harlequin book for every proof of purchase you have submitted with your request, plus a refund of the postage and handling charge you have included. Offer good in the U.S. and Canada only.

SLFW-SWPR

SILHOUETTE® OFFICIAL SWEEPSTAKES ENTRY FORM

4-FWSRS-3

Complete and return this Entry Form immediately – the more entries you submit, the better your chances of winning!

- Entries must be received by **December 31, 1991**.
- A Random draw will take place on **January 30, 1992**.
- No purchase necessary.

Yes, I want to win a FASHION A WHOLE NEW YOU Sensuous and Adventurous prize from Silhouette:

Name _____ Telephone _____ Age _____

Address _____

City _____ State _____ Zip _____

Return Entries to: **Silhouette FASHION A WHOLE NEW YOU,**
P.O. Box 9056, Buffalo, NY 14269-9056 © 1991 Harlequin Enterprises Limited

PREMIUM OFFER

To receive your free gift, send us the required number of proofs-of-purchase from any specially marked FASHION A WHOLE NEW YOU Silhouette or Harlequin Book with the Offer Certificate properly completed, plus a check or money order (do not send cash) to cover postage and handling payable to Silhouette FASHION A WHOLE NEW YOU Offer. We will send you the specified gift.

OFFER CERTIFICATE

Item	A. SENSUAL DESIGNER VANITY BOX COLLECTION (set of 4) *(Suggested Retail Price $60.00)*	B. ADVENTUROUS TRAVEL COSMETIC CASE SET (set of 3) *(Suggested Retail Price $25.00)*
# of proofs-of-purchase	18	12
Postage and Handling	$3.50	$2.95
Check one	☐	☐

Name _____

Address _____

City _____ State _____ Zip _____

Mail this certificate, designated number of proofs-of-purchase and check or money order for postage and handling to: **Silhouette FASHION A WHOLE NEW YOU Gift Offer,** P.O. Box 9057, Buffalo, NY 14269-9057. Requests must be received by December 31, 1991.

ONE PROOF-OF-PURCHASE

4-FWSRP-3

To collect your fabulous free gift you must include the necessary number of proofs-of-purchase with a properly completed Offer Certificate.

© 1991 Harlequin Enterprises Limited

See previous page for details.